SIMON & SCHUSTER CHILDR

ADVANCE READER

TITLE: The Bravest Warrior in Nefaria

AUTHOR: Adi Alsaid

IMPRINT: Aladdin

ON-SALE DATE: 09/05/2023

ISBN: 978-1-6659-2775-8

FORMAT: hardcover

PRICE: $18.99 US/$23.99 CAN

AGES: 8–12

PAGES: *304pp*

Please send any review or mention of this book to
ChildrensPublicity@simonandschuster.com.

Aladdin • Atheneum Books for Young Readers
Beach Lane Books • Beyond Words • Boynton Bookworks
Caitlyn Dlouhy Books • Denene Millner Books
Libros para niños • Little Simon • Margaret K. McElderry Books
MTV Books • Paula Wiseman Books • Salaam Reads
Simon & Schuster Books for Young Readers
Simon Pulse • Simon Spotlight

THE BRAVEST WARRIOR IN NEFARIA

ADI ALSAID

ALADDIN
NEW YORK   LONDON   TORONTO   SYDNEY   NEW DELHI

ALADDIN

An imprint of Simon & Schuster Children's Publishing Division

1230 Avenue of the Americas, New York, New York 10020

First Aladdin hardcover edition September 2023

Text copyright © 2023 by Adi Alsaid

Jacket illustration copyright © 2023 by Kristina Kister

For information about special discounts for bulk purchases, please contact Simon & Schuster Special Sales at 1-866-506-1949 or business@simonandschuster.com.

The Simon & Schuster Speakers Bureau can bring authors to your live event. For more information or to book an event contact the Simon & Schuster Speakers Bureau at 1-866-248-3049 or visit our website at www.simonspeakers.com.

Designed by Laura Lyn DiSiena & Irene Vandervoort

The text of this book was set in New Aster LT.

Manufactured in the United States of America 0723 FFG

2 4 6 8 10 9 7 5 3 1

Library of Congress Cataloging-in-Publication Data TK

ISBN 9781665927758 (hc)

ISBN 9781665927772 (ebook)

For Laura and Remy, as a bedtime story

PART I

1

THE KINGDOM OF NEFARIA was beautiful, but prone to evil schemes.

There was, for instance, the Great Cheese Fraud of the Fourteenth Century (the perpetrators made quite a bit of cheddar before the villagers caught on and tore them to shreds). Then there was Lord Maximilian's ill-fated attempt to control the land with highly trained spider monkeys (that the spider monkeys ended up being quite peaceful did not make the scheme any less evil). And who could forget the Anti-Beanbag Society's plan to slightly empty every beanbag in the land until none of them were comfortable?

The residents of Nefaria had grown used to schemes popping up, and though they tried to remain vigilant and refused to let their land go full-on evil, it was exhausting to always keep an eye out for these things. And hard, too. Sometimes the evilest of schemes don't seem all that evil at first glance. They seem normal, harmless—pleasant, even. They can take on the appearance of something commonplace, with no hint at the evil lurking beneath. Even the kingdom's dedicated evil sniff-er-outers missed a lot of them.

Some Nefarians left, of course, fleeing to the nearby king-doms of Jovialla and Los Angsteles. Even if a place is home, there's only so much people are willing to deal with. Other Nefarians tried to find a reason *why* their land was particu-larly prone to evil schemes. They tested the water, and the soil, and even some birds. But there wasn't anything demonstrably evil in any of them, and so a lot of people went on with their lives and hoped all the hubbub about evil schemes would fade away eventually.

Bobert Bougainvillea—a young and smallish resident of the upper hills of Nefaria—never really thought about evil schemes. Maybe because eleven-year-olds are usually not the ones called upon to fight them. Young Nefarians learned about evil schemes in school, and in the course of their daily lives (sometimes it seemed like it was all adults wanted to talk about), but Bobert himself thought of them as a part of the world that he didn't understand much but also didn't have to yet, kind of like taxes, or how to tell if fruit at the market was any good. Bobert also didn't think about evil schemes much because he was too busy dealing with other things that were borderline evil—or at least they felt that way to him.

Like waking up at sunrise to walk uphill, then downhill,

then back uphill to school. A beautiful hike, sure, as Nefaria was full of canyons, majestic in the morning light, or as majestic as anything could be at that time of day. But all the while Bobert had to avoid the flying goats (part of another failed evil scheme), which brayed way too loudly, and whose droppings splatted to the ground like the grossest bombs ever. And after an hour of huffing and puffing and ducking and diving, he had a whole day of classes to sit through with his clothes sweaty and his legs sore.

Then there were the other kids.

They never seemed to *see* him. If that was evil or not, Bobert couldn't tell. He didn't care much what it was called. He didn't like it.

When they worked on group projects, other students all rushed to find one another. Even the kids who were picked on found solace in one another. But Bobert was always left last, looking around, waiting for the teacher to try to direct the kid who hadn't gotten to his friends fast enough to join Bobert in a team. The other kid would be wandering around the classroom, counting off classmates, passing by Bobert two or three times until Bobert managed to raise his voice and say, "I don't have anyone."

At lunch he rotated seats, waiting for the day when someone would tell him he was too close. Tell him to get lost. Tell him to leave them alone. Even negative acknowledgment would have suited Bobert. But no. They never even looked his way. They sometimes sniffed at the air hungrily (his dad made Nefaria's best goat stew), but then they'd pretend it was one of their own meals that they were sniffing and Bobert would remain invisible.

After school, in no rush to begin his hour-long hike back home, Bobert would sometimes follow groups of schoolmates as they made their way into the woods to play, or as they went into town to cause mischief. He didn't even have to be particularly sneaky as he followed them. If he stepped on a twig, they might turn their heads over their shoulders to look back, but they never seemed to see him just a few yards behind. He could even whistle to himself, watching them intently, and it was as if he were a ghost.

Except even that wasn't true, because most of the kids at school talked to the various ghosts that lived in Nefaria. His classmates would talk to *ghosts* and not to him.

It had always been like this, as far as Bobert could remember. At the park when he was little, he was constantly digging holes in the sandbox by himself. In first grade he played hide-and-seek at recess, thrilled to be included, only to be found hours later, hiding in the gardening shed, by the school groundskeeper. All the kids had forgotten he was playing.

Now, there were rare little moments here and there when kids saw him, spoke to him, and when sometimes it even felt like he could have friends. Like the morning just a few months ago when he and Stanbert had talked about their favorite famous sword-swallowers before school. Or the time Rubyn had come over to do a class project with him and they actually spent the whole time laughing as they put their poster together, recounting their favorite exploits of the famous warrior Imogene Petunias.

But those were just brief glimpses of hope, and the next day at school Stanbert and Rubyn didn't look his way at all. Bobert would be left on his own to think about Nefaria's greatest living warrior, Imogene Petunias, pretending he was as popular and beloved as she was.

Once, Bobert asked his parents, the only people who seemed to see him all the time, why he was invisible to others. But one of the unfortunate things about parents, as anyone with them will tell you, is that they don't have all the answers. They sat beside him and tried to tell him it was all going to be okay, but they couldn't tell him why things weren't okay right now, or when it was going to stop being like this.

The day that Bobert stumbled into one of Nefaria's evil schemes started out just like all those others. Long, terrible, kinda pretty walk to school. Flying-goat poop. He pretended to be Imogene Petunias, fighting off warriors from Grumponia, in order to make the hike a little more interesting. No one said "hi" in the morning; no one said "that smells great" at lunch. There was a brief moment of excitement when he thought Candelabra, one of the coolest girls in school, had asked him for a quill. But it turned out she had been talking to Jennizabeth, who was sitting behind him.

His parents were going to be in town for a meeting until night, so instead of going home when school was over, Bobert decided he would go to the town square and sit in the sun and do his schoolwork. And maybe people *there* would notice him. Maybe someone would sit on a bench next to him and ask him about his day. If that didn't happen, at least he would be with his parents sooner, not having to wait for them to make it back home.

He took the path everyone from school took when they wanted to go to town: behind the main building, past the school's various pigpens, following the shadow of the turret on the berry fields, until he found the tree where the spider monkeys sold candies to the schoolchildren.

Bobert waved to the spider monkeys but didn't stop, appreciating the little head nod that the dad monkey gave him before Bobert slipped into the woods.

He'd taken his time leaving school, so he was surprised when he heard voices coming from just ahead. He picked up his pace, because sometimes just eavesdropping on other kids made him feel a little less alone.

"It's definitely not true," he heard one of the voices say, though he couldn't yet see who it was. There were at least three of them crunching their way through the leaves on the path. Nefaria didn't have four straightforward seasons. There were more like seventeen of them. But throughout most, the leaves were crunchy.

"It is!" a second voice exclaimed.

"If you think it's just a legend"—a third voice spoke up—"then why don't you go and do it?"

It was then that Bobert saw through the trees that it was Candelabra, Jennizabeth, and Stanbert. Unlike him, Candelabra seemed to be friends with everyone, easily jumping from friend group to friend group, universally liked. *How did she do it?*

She and Jennizabeth were walking in front, with Stanbert following behind. He was using a fallen branch like a walking stick, although he mostly just waved it around and swung it at tree trunks as he passed by.

"I don't even like gum that much," Jennizabeth said. "Plus, I've had gumballs from that machine a million times before. It's just a normal gumball machine. And you never get the red ones, which everyone knows are the best ones."

"I like the purple ones," Stanbert said.

Candelabra and Jennizabeth (and Bobert from afar) let their silence tell him how wrong he was.

"How come we don't know anyone who's disappeared, then?" Stanbert said after a moment.

"Because we're not dummies!" Candelabra said. "I don't know about you, but I don't have to stick my hand in a fire to learn that getting burned hurts. Someone learned that lesson for me a long time ago."

"Or we *are* dummies, because we believe some silly story without any evidence," Stanbert countered. "Don't you listen to what Professor Blort says? Believing something without evidence can feel good, but that doesn't mean that thing is true."

Bobert could only see their backs, but he could sense Candelabra rolling her eyes. He'd seen her roll her eyes in class a lot, especially in Professor Blort's class. He was one of those teachers who seemed to believe that everyone but him was wrong. He would probably become an Elder someday, Bobert thought. Along with the king, the Council of Elders helped decide how a lot of things in Nefaria ran. And they mostly thought every idea but theirs was bad, even if it was one of their own ideas from years before.

"Have you ever gotten a gumball after sundown?" Stanbert asked. He whacked at an overhead branch with his walking stick. Little bits of the branch fell off and landed on him, though he pretended like they hadn't.

"Well, no. But that's because my mom gets mad if I ruin my dinner," Jennizabeth answered.

"So, you have evidence that the gumball machine is normal during the day, but we all know that," Stanbert said. "What you don't have evidence of is that the machine is normal *after* sundown. I'm just saying we prove it."

They fell into silence again, the challenge hanging in the air, like a ghost. But less chatty than a ghost.

They continued on for a few minutes that way, each deep in thought, the only sound the wind rustling the leaves and their boots crunching down on the ground. Bobert liked it so much, walking a few steps behind them: the silence made him feel like he was part of the group too.

Bobert knew what gumball machine they were talking about. He'd heard the stories too (spoken near him, never to him). The rumors said that if you tried to get a gumball after sundown, the machine trapped you inside. But, as Stanbert had pointed out, no one had gotten trapped that he knew of. There weren't even *that* many unexplained disappearances in Nefaria. Most of them were because of the quicksand pits that hadn't been covered up.

Bobert vaguely remembered his parents talking about a kid they knew getting trapped in a gumball machine when they were little, but that was only once, and he couldn't even remember if it was a real memory or if he was getting confused with a rumor or—

Oof.

Too busy thinking about the machine and feeling like he was part of the group, Bobert failed to notice that they had stopped moving. Which resulted in him walking directly into Candelabra.

He was smaller than most kids in his grade, and Candelabra had already hit a growth spurt, so it was Bobert who ended up on his back on the ground. Looking up, briefly confused about what had happened, Bobert thought to himself that it was a really pretty day. Afternoons in Nefaria could be beautiful, what with the sun making the orange leaves glow, and no goats to be spotted in the super-blue sky. Goats usually took afternoon naps.

Then Candelabra's face blocked the view. He hadn't noticed her freckles before, or the way one nostril was a little bigger than the other.

"Were you following us?"

Bobert blinked. All three of them were looking at him now. It was a little intimidating. But also kind of a thrill.

"He ran right into you," Stanbert said. "Of course he was following us." He then gently poked at Bobert with his stick. "Why were you following us?"

"Bobert," Bobert said, hoping they would remember him if he said his name. That they would realize he'd been in school with them for years, had sat next to them in class and participated in projects alongside them.

"Whatever," Stanbert said. "Were you following us?"

Bobert gathered himself and stood back up. "I wasn't. I was just going into town."

"*We* were going into town," Jennizabeth said. "So you *were* following us."

"I was, uh, doing both?" Bobert mumbled.

Candelabra watched him for a while before she said, "You were listening to us, weren't you?"

Bobert's eyes went wide. "Whaaaaat? Noooo."

"What do *you* think? About the curse?" she asked Bobert.

Bobert was still having to gather himself from being spoken to directly. His heart did a little jig in his chest. "Hm?"

"The gumball machine," Candelabra said. "Do you believe the stories?"

Bobert examined his feet, wondering how he could so desperately want to talk to other people and yet not know at all what to say to them. "I dunno," he mumbled. As soon as he'd mumbled, though, something inside him stirred, like it was rejecting his urge to not say something wrong, to not say the thing that would turn him invisible. "We live in a weird place where almost anything is possible and schemes are everywhere. I don't know if the gumball machine is cursed or not, but I think it's super interesting that it *could* be."

He bit his lip, wondering if he had made a terrible mistake. They were all staring at him. Candelabra especially was holding his gaze, like she was studying him.

Finally Stanbert broke the silence by turning to Candelabra. "Whatever. The stories are not true! And we should stop being so scared and just use it."

The group of three started walking down the path again, and Bobert watched them go, feeling like, sure, it wasn't the best of exchanges, but he was sad it was over so quickly.

Then Candelabra looked over her shoulder at him. "Are you coming?"

2

DO YOU EVER WISH that sometimes days stopped at a certain point? Sunday, for example. You woke up late, then had your favorite sugary cereal (people often get the impression that Nefaria doesn't have sugary cereals, what with the flying goats and the evil schemes and the occasional wizard wreaking havoc on the land, but they're wrong). You got to read a book in the sun with no chores and there was the slightest bit of a breeze. Then your dad took you into town for ostrich burgers and cider ice cream, and he even took you into the play hall, where you got to shoot a bow and arrow at some balloons and you really channeled Imogene Petunias, so you did well enough to win a prize you'd been hoping to win for what felt like years now.

But then it was time to go back home, and do your Nefarian History homework, and tidy up your room, because you'd been making a mess of it all weekend. And you were cranky because of that, and a little bit sad, because you always got sad on Sunday evenings, what with Monday looming ahead, the threat of school and no one to talk to there. So, when your parents told you to go to bed and you wanted to play with your toy carts a little longer, you got into a fight and started yelling, so they punished you, and it felt like the whole day was ruined.

Wouldn't it have been better if, after you won the prize at the play hall, the world just saw what was coming and zipped ahead to the end of the day? Boom, you were asleep, and didn't have to deal with all that bad stuff still to come.

Well, Bobert knew that feeling. And he was about to feel it all over again, worse than he ever had before.

But Bobert was still feeling giddy that he was actually walking with some schoolmates. Far from wanting to jump forward in the day, Bobert wanted to slow it down. He wanted them to stay in his company, not look away and forget. He wasn't behind them, listening, *pretending* he was with them. He was actually *with* them. They were talking! And if he said something, it would fold into the rest of the conversation, as if he had always been a part of it.

"If you're so sure the stories are true," Stanbert was saying, the topic refusing to die, "then why don't you do it?"

"Aren't you listening to me?" Candelabra shot back. "It's *because* I believe they're true that I wouldn't dare try after sundown. I don't want to get trapped in a gumball machine."

"Yeah! If you're so sure it's safe," Jennizabeth said, giving

Stanbert a shove with her finger, "then *you* should have no problems doing it. Right, new kid?"

Bobert was not ready to be addressed so directly like that (even though he wasn't new at all). "Um," he said, because it was the only thing he could come up with.

"See, he thinks so too," Jennizabeth said.

"I don't think anyone should use the gumball machine!" Candelabra cried out, a little more aggressively than Bobert would have expected.

There was a heavy pause as her friends turned to her, and Bobert wondered if this was normal in their friendship. He felt a pang of sorrow that he was still on the outside looking in, but then Stanbert made a little snorting sound, which pulled Bobert from his thoughts. "Well, I think we should."

They were coming to the end of the path now, toward the edge of town, and the bustle of the market, the calls of vendors hawking their meats and fabrics and potions, were becoming clearer. He couldn't see them yet, but beyond the market there were lines and lines of squat buildings, most of them the homes of people who worked as staff in the various castles in the area. Would the group naturally split apart when they got to town? Probably they would. Any moment now they would forget Bobert; he was sure of it.

But maybe he could talk to them at school tomorrow. Maybe—and all of this was wild hope, he knew—Candelabra lived not too far away from him. Maybe she would start walking to school with him in the mornings. Maybe she had good tactics for avoiding falling goat poop, and she would show him all of them.

This was something his brain often did: trick him into hope. Trick him into thinking it could be different all of a sudden.

"So, what are we gonna do until then?" Stanbert said.

"Until when?" Bobert said.

"Until sundown," Stanbert said cheerfully, as if they were talking about catching a show at the amphitheater.

"I never said I was going to do it!" Jennizabeth protested.

Stanbert kind of waved his hand at her. "Well, you've been talking about it so much, *someone's* gonna have to, or this whole day will feel like it's been wasted."

Candelabra turned to Bobert, and it seemed like she wanted to change the subject. "What were you coming into town for?"

"Um," he said again. His chances of having people continue to talk to him would probably be really low if he just kept saying the same thing over and over again. "I was gonna do homework at the square," he said. "My parents are going to some meeting thing, so I was gonna wait for them and then walk home with them. And hopefully they'll buy me some flower juice."

"You like that stuff?" Stanbert asked, wrinkling his nose. "It tastes like dirt."

Bobert's heart dropped. Any moment now they'd keep going, forget to look back.

"I like flower juice," Candelabra said. Then she sighed. "If we're waiting for sundown—which I think is a terrible idea, but whatever—it'd be good if I had all my homework done too."

They had broken through the trees now and could see the town clearly ahead of them, and slightly below. The town was set in one of Nefaria's many valleys, beautifully surrounded by huge mountains that made it hard for enemies to attack them, but also made the sun set a little earlier than everyone would have otherwise wanted.

Bobert wanted to keep talking to Candelabra about flower juice, and what kind she liked best, and who she thought had the best in town. But they'd reached the grassy part of the hill, and everyone knew that when you reached the grassy part of the hill, all conversation officially ended, and rolling began.

Jennizabeth was the first to throw herself down, and Bobert could barely believe what a good roller she was. She seemed to be in perfect control of herself, even though she was going faster than anyone he had ever seen.

Stanbert went right after her, a lot clumsier, but he was getting some good bounces along the way that looked fun. A little painful, but rolling down the hill wasn't really fun without a little pain.

This might have been the point when Bobert, later, would

have hoped the day could just zip ahead to bedtime, and not leave any chance for bad stuff to sneak into the day. But we never really know when that point in a day comes, do we? We just keep living the day forward, hoping the good times will keep going all the way through. And when times are good, when we have people who invite us to roll down a hill with them, how could we possibly fast-forward through that?

"You coming?" Candelabra asked him for the second time. She barely waited for him to nod before she was off, and Bobert threw himself down after her, smiling the whole way down.

NOT TOO FAR FROM TOWN, there was a castle.

And in the castle was a wizard named Matt. At that moment, Matt was in his lonely turret, looking out the window at the town square and petting his mangy, long-haired cat, Justin. Justin didn't love being petted, but he was old and grumpy and too comfortable to move, so instead he occasionally chewed on Matt's hand and kept on purring.

Matt let the cat chew, every now and then reminding Justin about their many exploits. Right now he was recounting the time he'd tried to freeze everyone in the kingdom with a blizzard so he could stage a coup. The way Justin remembered it, the wizard had only made it kind of chilly for a weekend.

That plan had failed, but any day now, this one was going to succeed.

Matt stared at the distant plaza, at the gumball machine he had placed in its specific corner of the square so he could study it all night from his favorite spot in his castle. For what felt like forever, he'd been sitting there, watching, waiting for people to fall into his trap.

Sure, it had been a very long time of waiting, and he sort of regretted the whole they-only-get-trapped-in-the-machine-after-sundown thing. At first it seemed like the right approach: he wanted to build his army without raising too much suspicion. If he made it so everyone who got a gumball from his machine got stuck inside, then people would absolutely notice. There'd be a whole mess of witnesses, and they'd quickly discover that the gumball machine was to blame. The kingdom's evil-scheme sniffer-outers (many kids were disappointed when they learned that they were just detectives and not some sort of animals that could sniff out evil) would investigate, and since the gumball machine was one of the first of its kind, it would have been really easy to trace back to Matt.

So he had added the after-sundown clause. Plus, during the day it seemed like the gumball machine attracted more children than adults, which could be an issue. Both ethically and for the purposes of having an army good enough to take over the kingdom.

Unfortunately, it turned out that very few adults were interested in gumball machines, even after dark. The first week, only two people fell into the trap, and they were both kids. Matt thought about letting them go and starting over, but setting up magical traps was exhausting, and the gumball machine had been really expensive.

A deeply lazy person, Matt decided to just stick with it and see what happened. A week went by before he noticed a surprising calm in town. It hit him that there hadn't been any search parties, there'd been no breaking-news gatherings in the plaza, no posters on the lampposts. Even after a third kid fell into the trap, the town went on as before.

After two more quiet months, an adult used the gumball machine. A very childish adult, sure, but fully grown. This time there *was* a bit of a stir about town, and several search parties. But some of the search-party members fell into quicksand traps, so those were abandoned pretty quickly, thankfully. Still, there was more hubbub than was comfortable for Matt, especially considering he had only managed to get one adult and three kids so far. When the king's army was about to get called in, Matt released the childish adult, and things immediately calmed down, as if there weren't still some children missing.

So Matt went back and looked at the spell he had cast again and realized he'd read it too quickly and flubbed some of the words, which had made it so that any kids who were trapped were forgotten. But the more he thought about it, the more that felt like an even better plan now. He didn't really like the idea of battle, after all. Swords clanging were annoyingly loud. Blood and guts were gross. And if there was even a slight chance of Matt himself getting hurt, that didn't sound like any fun at all.

Having kids march to the castle? Who would even fight them? Knights would happily fight against an army of entranced men and women. But would they fight back against an eight- or nine-year-old, even if that child were pointing a sword straight at them? Matt would bet they wouldn't. Plus, it would make the people of Nefaria more willing to accept his rule if he took over peacefully. So being peaceful in overthrowing the current regime seemed like a smart idea. Especially if he wanted them to throw him a parade for his coronation. Because what fun would it be without a parade?

Matt simply had to wait for more kids to fall into the trap.

But, it turned out, not a lot of kids actually went out after dark. And those who did were sometimes specifically forbidden to ruin their dinner with those fancy new gumballs. Weeks went by before another kid came at dark, and she emptied out her pockets, found nothing, and continued on her way.

So Matt waited. And waited. And waited. He brainstormed other ways to make his scheme move along faster, but his ideas had dried up, and he was really invested in the gumball machine working. He did think about just flat-out kidnapping the two hundred or so children he needed for the plan work, but that didn't feel like the way a wizard would do things. He wasn't a common criminal, after all!

Something many people often forget—but most Nefarians don't—is that evil people almost never think they're evil.

He tried to tweak the sundown provision, but it was one of those spells that was kind of like a bad sticker. Once it stuck, it was impossible to peel off and restick somewhere else without leaving a gross, white residue behind. So Matt waited. He was nothing if not patient.

But then something truly magical happened—rumors of the few disappearances started to swirl, and that only tempted more children to try the machine. Matt sat back and watched his army grow.

It had now been years since his plan was set in motion, and he was so close. He just needed one more kid, his wizard math told him. Wizard math, as any kid in Nefaria will tell you, is the hardest math there is, but it was one of Matt's few natural talents.

He petted Justin, who bit down on a knuckle. He stared out the window at the town square, begging kids to hold on to their coins until sundown. His other pet, Camila, a parrot he'd acquired during his brief stint as a pirate, flew onto the windowsill. She turned her head to Matt and smirked. "Any biters today?"

"Shut up," he grumbled.

He could see a group of kids sitting on a bench across from the gumball machine, which seemed promising, but Matt had learned not to get his hopes up.

They did occasionally walk over to the machine and inspect

it, but had yet to slip a silver nefickle into its slot. Matt imagined that they were talking about the curse, the way kids did so often. But talking wasn't going to help Matt build his army.

If only kids these days would stop being so cautious.

You may ask: What did Matt want to do with this army? Matt the Wizard wanted what so many evil people before him wanted: *more*. He wanted more power, more wealth, more recognition. He wanted all of Nefaria in his hands, if he could have it (shrinking it down was another one of his failed schemes). He wanted to be able to go wherever he pleased without getting weird looks, without someone saying "no," or "get out of here," or "What's that smell?"

Matt cleared his throat and stood up. Justin let out a complaining meow as he hopped down to the floor. "I need a snack," Matt said, though he wasn't exactly hungry. There was just a little empty space inside him, and he was going to fill it with food. "Let me know if something exciting happens."

4

"CAN I BORROW YOUR ERASER?" Candelabra asked Bobert.

They were all sitting on a bench in the main square, across from the gumball machine. Bobert had never done homework with other kids before, and it was strange how much he liked it.

For a while now, they had stopped talking about the gumball machine and the curse. They sat in the sun and talked about school. They all agreed that the worst meal the cafeteria served was fish sticks, since they were more like fish noodles. They all liked fish and they all liked noodles, but noodles made out of fish just weren't the right move. They disagreed about the best meal the cafeteria served (one vote each for pizza, crunchy potatoes, and bone broth, and Bobert voted for spicy green things that no one could identify).

Then they pulled out their bound notebooks and quills and started working. Bobert and Candelabra sat side by side on the bench, while Stanbert and Jennizabeth splayed out on the ground, ignoring the weird looks that adults passing by cast their way.

Bobert kept expecting the others to look at him in surprise, wondering where he'd come from. But whatever magical spell had been cast on the afternoon lingered on.

It was one of the best days Bobert had had in a long time, and he didn't even feel disappointed when a squirrel messenger came by with a message from his parents. Apparently, the meeting—a weekly town hall they never missed, since they said it was important to be involved—was going to run late into the night. So he wouldn't get flower juice like he was hoping, or have company on his walk home.

But he had had this afternoon, and the knowledge of it would keep him company at least until bedtime, he was sure of it. As would the hope that this was just the start. That he had friends now, or at least people who would look his way at school. The invisibility he'd been cursed with was over, as inexplicably as it had begun.

Bobert had the sudden urge to tell them all these thoughts, to tell them that he would do anything to stay visible. But he knew that might sound weird and a little intense, and so he kept quiet and passed Candelabra his eraser.

Then the sun started dipping toward the mountains, and all of them stared quietly across the square at the gumball machine. Bobert wondered who was going to bring it up again. It definitely wasn't going to be him. And he had a feeling Candelabra was avoiding the topic too, as if she was hoping everyone else had forgotten about it.

Jennizabeth finally spoke up as she was coloring in a map for her geography class. "Do you guys think the curse kicks in when the sun is below the mountains, or only when it's below the horizon *behind* the mountains?"

"Only one way to find out!" Stanbert said, looking pointedly at Candelabra.

"That's not true—there's tons of ways," she mumbled. "None of us should use the machine. This is a bad idea." Her voice got quiet, and Bobert wondered why she seemed to be afraid. She didn't strike him as the kind of girl to be afraid often.

"Other than trying it, what other ways are there?" Stanbert said.

Candelabra didn't have anything to say to that, but Bobert decided to help his new friend out a little. He hoped that thinking of Candelabra as his new friend wasn't going to jinx him in any way. "Well, you could technically ask whoever did the curse if it's real. That'd be another way."

"True," Stanbert conceded. "But since we don't know who did the curse, that's not much of an option."

Again, the challenge in Stanbert's words was silent, but Bobert could feel it, and he knew the others felt it too. Oh, feeling things with others, as a group. What a great feeling *that* was.

Stanbert wasn't going to let it stay silent, though. He turned to Jennizabeth and spoke the words they all knew were coming. "I dare you."

A flock of pigeons took off nearby, their wings flapping all at once, causing an ominous whoosh to flow through the square.

Stanbert raised an eyebrow at Jennizabeth. "So?"

"So, what?"

"Do you accept my dare?"

"Stanbert," Candelabra said. "I'm not joking. We shouldn't mess with it."

"I dared Jennizabeth, not you."

Jennizabeth looked at her feet. She kicked at a pigeon feather that had landed by the bench.

Bobert suddenly felt very bad for Jennizabeth, and the dilemma she'd talked herself into. It was entirely possible to not believe in a curse and still be scared of it. And it was reasonable of Stanbert to try to push Jennizabeth toward the gumball machine, because either way, he won. Either he was right and he was safe, or he was wrong and everyone was safe. But it wasn't really fair.

Before he could even think about what he was saying or why, Bobert said, "I'll do it."

The other three turned to him, their expressions a mix of shock and awe and curiosity. Bobert let his eyes meet Candelabra's longest. He didn't know why, but he felt calm. Maybe he didn't believe in curses at all. At least not anymore. Maybe he was just happy to be visible, and would do anything to stay that way.

"Bobert, no," Candelabra finally said, her voice almost at a whisper.

"I can do it," Bobert repeated, emboldened by the fact that Candelabra remembered his name. His name!

"You don't have to," Candelabra said.

"It's okay," Bobert said, feeling more confident than he probably should have been. It's funny how good days and good feelings can sometimes carry us through moments we might have thought we wouldn't be able to handle. "I'll do it—I'll use the gumball machine after dark."

There was a long pause; then Stanbert asked, "What do you think will happen?" The bravado was gone from his voice.

Bobert just shrugged. It hardly seemed like the most important matter to think about, the consequences. Whatever happened, he felt certain that if he was the one to test the machine, Candelabra, Stanbert, and Jennizabeth would not be so quick to forget him. It was like a magical solution to all his problems, and they were offering it up so conveniently.

He looked down at his History of Magic homework, as if

just now realizing that it was almost finished. He dipped his quill in the inkpot they were all sharing, but when he looked down at his sheet of paper, his eyes refused to read the words on the page. Not knowing what else to do, he started to doodle in the margins.

"Something doesn't feel right," Candelabra said, but her voice wasn't as resolute as normal, and no one knew what to say to that.

The sun was definitely down behind the mountains at that point, the chill in the air confirming that it was no longer day out. Whether the sun had fully set wasn't clear. He supposed it would just have to be up to the supposed curse to decide.

He folded up his notebook and tucked his quill into his bag. Then he couldn't decide whether to leave the bag with Candelabra and the rest, or take it with him, and so he held it on his lap for an awkward moment. The others seemed to notice his movement, so before it got too weird, he stood and threw the bag's strap over his shoulder.

"You're really gonna go?" Jennizabeth asked.

"I think it's technically sundown now," he said. He started walking toward the gumball machine. He wondered if the others would follow him, but he didn't have to wonder for long. They were on his heels in no time.

If someone had asked him at that moment, like they would

later on, what he was thinking as he approached the machine, he supposed he would say that it just felt like everything was going to be all right.

The square was mostly empty now. Nefaria got cold quickly, especially at that time of year. People were headed home to light fires and prepare dinner, to watch their favorite programs on the wizard screens most people had in their living rooms. Maybe if it had been another day, if the town hall regarding all the monkey business hadn't been happening, there would have been someone around to stop him. Someone who maybe remembered, even if vaguely, that one time someone had gone missing after being seen at the gumball machine.

Bobert dug into his pocket for the nefickle he'd been occasionally fingering throughout the day, checking to make sure it was still there. He pulled it out and laid it flat in the palm of his hand. What a small price to pay for friendship.

He stared into the gumball machine, all those little globules of color. The others crowded around him, watching Bobert more than the machine itself. Bobert was looking as closely as possible, trying to spot anything that might have been strange about it. But it looked totally normal: just a big glass bowl full of gumballs, with a little mechanism for inserting the coin at the front, and a knob to turn until the gumball popped out of the slot at the bottom.

"You sure you want to do this?" Candelabra asked.

"What do we tell people if you disappear?" Stanbert said.

Bobert shrugged. "I don't think I will. But . . . if I don't, do you guys want to . . ." He swallowed, not sure if just saying the words aloud would make it all fall away: the progress he'd made with these three classmates, the joy he'd felt all afternoon. "Do you guys want to hang out again?"

He stared at the gumballs as he said this. If he had been able to raise his gaze toward the others, he would have seen Candelabra smile. She was the first to say, "Yes."

He looked at Stanbert, trying to read in his eyes if he remembered the last time they'd talked. If he was planning on forgetting Bobert again.

"Sure," he said, giving nothing else away. Jennizabeth nodded quietly beside him.

That was enough for Bobert. He slipped the coin into the machine's slot, and, giving his new friends one last look, he turned the knob.

He heard the clunk of the coin entering the machine, and then the soft rumbling of the gumballs inside shifting. Completely normal gumball-machine behavior. Now Bobert was going to have a gumball and three new friends.

Then, a pause.

Like the world was deciding what to do. Like the curse was

looking at the sky and the amount of light in it and determining whether it was technically sundown or not. Like it could have gone either way.

There was a swirl of gumball-colored light, and Bobert was gone.

5

BOBERT WAS GONE only to the outside world. While Candelabra, Stanbert, and Jennizabeth blinked at one another and tried to remember what they were doing, Bobert opened his eyes, as if from a brief nap. But one of those brief naps that completely messes with your sense of time and place and makes you confused about which world you've woken up into. You know the kind.

Everything around Bobert was a slight shade of green, like he was seeing the world through strange glasses. He stood up, since it seemed like he was lying down. He didn't remember doing that, but he couldn't remember what he'd been doing just a few minutes before, either. Everything smelled kinda nice, too. Like sour apple, maybe. Or was it watermelon?

He took a step forward, tripped on his backpack, and immediately hit a wall.

"Ooh, six seconds!" a muffled voice called out. "Who had six seconds?"

A chorus of muffled voices responded. Bobert rubbed his nose, which was throbbing, and blinked away the tears that sprang up in his eyes. He pressed his palms into them, trying to make sense of what had just happened.

"Shh, everyone. The timer's still going."

"Shut up, Daveffery! That's practically cheating."

"I didn't say anything," the first voice said. "Look, he's barely listening."

Finally, Bobert was able to gather himself enough to look around. He noticed now that just beyond the green wall—it was actually more like tinted glass, though softer—there were a bunch of round, colorful globes. And inside each of those globes there was a kid.

Some of the kids were a little younger than him, some a little older. Some were dressed funny, like in portraits of people from the past.

"Here it comes!" a husky feminine voice said.

"Stop helping!"

Bobert wanted to walk again, but he'd learned his lesson. He stuck his arms out in front of him instead, feeling for the wall. He was aware of all those faces looking in his direction, and he scanned around, meeting their gazes, feeling a little bit like an animal in a zoo. Which meant he would have to reexamine his feelings about zoos, but maybe after he figured out what was happening to him.

The other kids kept saying things to one another, things Bobert could understand linguistically, even if he couldn't make sense of their meaning at all. He decided that before he could deal with all of them and what was happening to him and what *had* happened to him, he had to figure out the weird wall surrounding him. Because it wasn't just in front of him; it was all around.

That was when it hit him.

Actually, it had already hit his nose. But now was when it hit his brain: the gumball machine. The curse. It was true.

And now he was inside the machine. He was inside a gumball.

He abandoned his plan to inspect the wall and sat down.

"Wow, less than a minute," the husky feminine voice said.

"Shut up, you don't know that he knows yet."

"Sure I do," she responded. "Hey, kid, do you know where you are?"

Bobert put his head in his hands and took a few deep breaths the way his mom had taught him when he was little and used to have nightmares. Maybe this was a nightmare, and if he breathed long and deeply enough, when he raised his head again he'd be back in the town square with Candelabra and the others.

"Did anyone bet on whether he would puke?"

A whole bunch of voices called back that they had, which

made it really hard for Bobert to think that he could open his eyes and everything would be normal again. Or better than normal.

He took another breath, then looked up. Yup. Green world. A bunch of other spheres, with kids wearing outdated clothes inside them.

Even though he had never once in his life gulped before, because that was something people didn't do in real life, Bobert gulped.

"I'm in the gumball machine."

Back outside the gumball machine, in the town square, Candelabra, Stanbert, and Jennizabeth blinked at one another. Somewhere nearby, the wind caused an open door to slam shut, which scared one of the goats flying overhead, and it pooped right on Stanbert's shoulder.

As Stanbert flicked the poop off his shoulder, the three seemed to realize that they had no idea what they were doing there.

"What are we doing here?" Jennizabeth asked.

They all looked at the gumball machine. Candelabra realized there was a pink eraser in her hand, which she didn't remember having. Then something seemed to click for Stanbert.

"Nice try," he said to Jennizabeth. "You're not gonna get out of the dare so easily."

Candelabra didn't chime in, looking back and forth from the gumball machine to the eraser. When she turned it over, she saw a name written on the back. *Bobert.* A weird feeling started to creep along her spine.

"I never said yes to a dare," Jennizabeth mumbled. "Did I?"

"Why else are we here?" Stanbert said.

There was a loud commotion behind them. The town hall had just ended, and apparently the adults were quite fired up about whatever had been discussed. Two men were yelling at a well-dressed spider monkey in a suit, who just sauntered past them. "There's too much monkey business in this town!" one of the men yelled.

Candelabra blocked them out and racked her brain, trying to figure out why she felt so weird, why the last few hours felt a little bit like a dream. She looked over her shoulder at the route they'd taken from the school, as if trying to see a past version of herself.

Memories came back to her: images of walking through the woods, laughing, talking about the supposed curse. How come they had hung out at the plaza? They spent almost every day after school together, sometimes at one another's houses, sometimes just playing in the woods with other kids from school. But they never came to the plaza. She looked at the eraser again, wondering who Bobert was, how she came to have that little pink oval in her hand.

When she looked up, she saw that Stanbert and Jennizabeth were looking at her, wanting her to settle the matter. Instead of saying anything, Candelabra started searching through her pockets. Her friends looked at her, sure that she wasn't doing what they thought she was doing.

When she found nothing in her pockets, Candelabra slung her backpack over her shoulder and started zipping it open to rummage through, knowing that somewhere in there was a coin.

"Um," Jennizabeth said. "Are you doing what I think you're doing?"

"And why?" Stanbert added.

"I don't know," Candelabra said honestly. "Something feels off. Like we're missing something." She looked up at them. "Don't you feel that?"

They shrugged, starting to look a little more worried than confused.

Candelabra didn't pay them any attention, sure she had a nefickle somewhere in her bag. She pulled out her pencil case, where she sometimes kept loose change, and accidentally pulled out something else. It was a large yellow envelope that she didn't recognize, and instead of going straight to her pencil case, she was moved by curiosity to open it.

Their class portraits. There were the individual portraits of her that her mom always liked to hang up on their icebox, and then one of the entire class.

As Stanbert and Jennizabeth started arguing about the curse again, Candelabra studied the class portrait. Then she looked back at the eraser, and that name, Bobert. It didn't ring a bell, but when she looked at the list of names written at the bottom of the portrait, there it was.

She scanned her classmates' faces until she came across one she couldn't recognize. He was a short, fair-skinned kid with floppy brown curls and a goofy smile that looked like either the portrait artist hadn't captured it very well, or this Bobert kid was bad at holding a smile for portraits.

Why couldn't she remember him, then? Maybe he had moved early in the year? But then how did she have his eraser? The more questions that occurred to her, the more two little words came up as the answer: "evil scheme." She thought of her sister, Sandraliere, stuck where she was, and felt the familiar gut punch of guilt.

"Do you remember a kid named Bobert?" Candelabra said, interrupting her friends' arguing.

"Can you be more specific?" Jennizabeth answered. "That's a super-common name."

Candelabra held up the portrait, and her friends came closer to get a better look.

THE BRAVEST WARRIOR IN NEFARIA

"Never seen him," Stanbert said.

"That's from this year?" Jennizabeth asked, furrowing her brow.

"Yeah."

"I bet even *he'd* be willing to test the machine," Stanbert said to Jennizabeth, and they started arguing again.

Something wasn't right. Candelabra was great at remembering names. She was popular exactly because she was friendly with everyone, got along with people who didn't have a lot of other friends.

What any of this had to do with the gumball machine, Candelabra didn't know. But something told her she had to find out. Like her own farts, Candelabra could smell an evil scheme before others could.

She had, after all, survived one not that long ago.

Candelabra tucked away the class portrait and zipped open her pencil case, where she found three nefickles. She stood up and approached the machine, playing with the coins in her hand.

The sound they made in her palm once again snapped Stanbert and Jennizabeth out of their arguing about the curse.

"Are you sure?" Jennizabeth said, rushing to Candelabra's side.

Candelabra didn't answer for a moment, staring at the machine, still trying to figure it all out. "This is all part of a scheme, I think."

"Um, yeah, a scheme that includes a cursed gumball machine that we shouldn't play with. No matter what Stanbert says," she said, shooting their friend a pointed look. Stanbert rolled his eyes.

Candelabra gave them both a serious glance, though, and Jennizabeth understood right away what Candelabra meant by it. Not everyone at school knew what Candelabra had gone through, but her closest friends knew that if there was even a hint of an evil scheme around, she was going to do what she could to stop it.

Candelabra closed her eyes and moved the nefickle toward the machine.

But it was already too late.

Candelabra had closed her eyes as the coin entered the slot. But instead of the clink of the coin slipping into the hidden machinery, she heard the nefickle hit the ground and roll away.

The adults across the plaza quieted down at the sound as if it were much louder. They looked over, wondering what those kids were up to. They didn't notice right away, the way Stanbert and Jennizabeth did, that the gumball machine that had stood in this particular corner of Nefaria for decades was no longer there.

ALMOST AS SOON AS BOBERT STARTED to wrap his head around the fact that he was inside the gumball machine, things changed once again. The sound of the other kids talking fell away. The green tint to the world, the other colorful globes, the gumball walls, even the backpack at his feet—they all disappeared.

Then the air was fresh again. Like he was outside. A quick look up confirmed that the night sky was directly above him, nothing else in the way. He was standing in a stone courtyard, and around him were what seemed like hundreds of other kids. They were still dressed in their outdated clothes. But they weren't looking at him anymore. They were looking at everything else, like he was. And they looked just as confused as Bobert was, maybe even more.

He studied his surroundings a little more closely. The courtyard was quite large, and it seemed to form a part of a compound, like the property surrounding a castle. It was dark, so it was hard to really discern what all the shadows were. But there was definitely a building nearby, and Bobert could make out a handful of windows with candlelight flickering behind them. Beyond the castle were the far-off shapes of mountains. It was impossible for him to be sure, but he thought they looked somewhat familiar: the mountains he had grown up in his whole life.

So he was back out in Nefaria? Had he just been really lucky, and the curse had been broken almost as soon as he'd fallen into it? Or was his invisibility a curse that had somehow canceled out the gumball machine's curse?

He turned to the girl who was standing next to him. She was about his age, maybe a little older (or she had already hit her growth spurt, unlike Bobert). She had two long braids, dark skin, and green nail polish that had mostly chipped away. Her clothes weren't quite as old-fashioned as some, and she wasn't crying like some of the others. "Where are we?" Bobert asked her.

She startled at his voice, as if she hadn't noticed there was anyone else around her. Which was disappointing. Even when he was cursed, he was invisible. Then she seemed to place him. "You're the new kid."

He nodded. "Do you know what's happening? Is this part of the gumball machine?"

She shook her head. "This is new," she said, her husky voice immediately familiar, assuring Bobert that she had been in there with him just a moment ago. She swallowed loudly, and bit the corner of her bottom lip, hard enough that Bobert wondered how it wasn't hurting her. "This is the first new thing that's happened in so long."

Bobert wanted to ask more, but she seemed to slip deep into thought again. A lot of the kids were doing just that, like they were frozen in place. Some others, though, were running around, maybe trying to find an exit. If that was what they were doing, they weren't succeeding. Bobert saw one tall kid with a big bushy hairdo trace the whole perimeter of the courtyard, then return to where he'd been standing. He was yelling something as he ran, too. "Get me out of here!"

Bobert looked for Candelabra and the others, but it didn't seem like they had been sucked into the machine or wherever he was. He looked up to the castle, thinking maybe he could find another clue there. That was when he saw movement in one of the turrets.

In the flickering candlelight of the topmost window, someone was bending over, then dashing across the window, carrying something, throwing it down again. Bobert was reminded of what it felt like to wake up a little too late and have to rush to get dressed and go to school.

The person, who had long hair and was possibly wearing a pointy hat, finally disappeared from the window. Bobert could trace their silhouette as they descended the turret, passing by the candlelit windows every few seconds, even more frantically than when they were up in their room.

The other kids seemed to notice it too, because a hush fell over the courtyard, which just a moment ago had been almost boisterous with chatter, cries, and screams.

Now that it was quiet, Bobert could hear the hurried foot-steps of the person going down the turret. They had a deep and raspy voice, and Bobert could tell because they kept yelling at someone named Camila. It was easy to tell where the person would emerge, and the now-silent group of kids moved their eyes toward the large wooden double doors that Bobert could now make out in the dark.

Just a few seconds later the doors burst open, and a man stumbled out, holding a torch in one hand. He was wearing a large, pointy hat, as Bobert had guessed, and he had long, gray hair, matted and somewhat greasy, along with a hefty beard: all telltale signs of a wizard.

But the parrot that flew behind the wizard and landed on his shoulder was confusing. Wizards famously kept cats as pets, not parrots. Bobert remembered having a coloring book when he was in kindergarten with a bunch of well-known wiz-ards in it. This one looked like someone who had been colored outside the lines.

Bobert held his breath, wondering if he was a good wizard who had rescued them from the gumball machine and just happened to be very disheveled, or if he was the evil type and had trapped them. Actually, it felt like everyone around him was holding their breath, waiting to see what this wizard would say.

But they were going to have to wait, because the wizard now stood in front of them, panting. He raised one finger, giving the multi-universal signal for *gimme a second*.

He cast a quick spell on his torch so that it would float near him while he put both his hands on his hips and doubled over to breathe deeper. Then he raised his arms behind his head and looked up at the sky, another multi-universal move that Bobert's PE teacher always had them do, even though no one (in any universe) was really sure it worked. "I wasn't ready," the wizard said.

Bobert turned to the girl with the braids to see if maybe she knew what was happening. She shrugged her shoulders. Funny that among all this, it still felt good to be acknowledged like that, to share a moment with someone else.

"Too fast," the wizard said, wheezing. "I ran too fast. Ohhh, way too fast." The parrot at his shoulder gave a squawk, but it kind of sounded like a laugh. "Shut up, bird." The wizard swatted at it, but it flapped its wings and flew out of reach.

Finally the wizard stood up straight. "Hello, children! I am the great wizard Matt!" He said his name with a lot of flair, waving his hands around as he did. Then he held his arms out and paused.

The kids shifted on their feet. Someone coughed. Bobert wondered whether he should applaud, but no one else was doing it, so he kept his arms by his sides.

"Nothing? The Great and Evil Wizard Matt? Purveyor of Wicked Wands? Chillest Wizard, Master of Blizzards? The Once and Future Cat Lord?"

If crickets existed in Nefaria, Bobert would have been able to hear them chirping. But they famously didn't have crickets, just singing mountain spiders, and Bobert could definitely hear them in the distance warming up for the night.

Matt the Wizard dropped his arms by his sides. "You have really never heard of me?"

A few kids were brave enough to say "no" out loud, but most just shook their heads. Bobert almost felt guilty about never having heard of him, but the guy had just called himself evil, so maybe it was good that Bobert had no idea who he was.

Matt sighed and grabbed hold of the floating torch again. "Well, soon enough everyone will know my name." He cleared his throat and stood up straighter. "As I was saying! I am the Great Wizard Matt. You may have already guessed that I am the reason you're here." He chuckled to himself in what Bobert was pretty sure was supposed to be an evil way, but it mostly sounded like Matt was trying not to cough. "That's right—I am the one who cursed the gumball machine that has kept you trapped all these years," Matt said. "Except you."

As he did, he pointed. The crowd naturally parted to see where Matt's finger was pointing, and that created a perfect path leading from Matt to Bobert. It was immediately the most attention Bobert had ever had in his life. Everyone was looking at him, and Bobert couldn't help but look behind him to make sure Matt wasn't pointing at someone else.

"You, child, were the last one I needed." Matt started walking toward Bobert, slowly and purposefully, his long, blue robe dragging on the ground behind him. "I've been waiting for so long to finally get enough of you, and now the time has come. *My* time has come."

He was getting closer and closer to Bobert, and Bobert's mouth started to go dry. And even though the wizard was talking to all the kids, Bobert felt right at the center of *everyone*'s attention. He was sweating and blushing at the same time, while also feeling like he might throw up.

Now Matt was close enough that Bobert could really get a good look at him: his ruddy cheeks, his beady eyes, the gray tangled hair beneath his hat and mixing with his beard, which grew almost to his large belly. He was really sweaty. But Bobert was too, so maybe it was just hotter out than he'd realized.

"So, thank you, my boy," Matt said, now close enough to touch Bobert. Which was exactly what he did next, reaching out a hand to hold Bobert's chin in his thumb and forefinger. "You, as the two hundredth fool to fall into my trap, have finally given me what I want."

There was a heavy pause in the air. It was the girl with the husky voice, the one next to Bobert, who said it out loud. "What *do* you want?"

Matt held on to Bobert's chin one moment longer, looking deep into his eyes. Bobert could see not just a strange twinkle in them, but all sorts of twinkles. All the evil thoughts that Matt had had throughout his life, all his schemes and tricks and spells, they were all right there. Something else, too, though— something almost familiar. Bobert wanted to shudder, but he just stood there and held his breath.

Finally Matt pulled his hand away and turned to address all of them at once. "You, children, are now my very own personal army. And you're going to help me take over Nefaria."

7

THE EVIL WIZARD MATT kept speaking for a while, every now and then pausing to leave room for applause or laughter, which never came. It was a tough crowd.

Eventually his spiel was done and he went inside to order scorpion pizza for everyone. Everyone knows an underfed army cannot fight. At least that was what all the books about overthrowing monarchies that Matt had in his library said.

Meanwhile, he'd directed the kids to each grab a sleep sack from the huge pile in the corner. They'd be sleeping in the courtyard to help toughen them up (although it really was quite lovely out, and a good chunk of kids in Nefaria slept outdoors most nights anyway). Then, in the morning, the battle would begin. He warned them not to even think about trying to escape, since there were "a whole bunch of spells" preventing them from doing that.

Not even Bobert believed that, and he usually listened to everything adults said. So it wasn't surprising that, as soon as

Matt made that announcement and turned to go back into the castle, everyone tried to run for the nearest exit.

They seemed to arrive at this decision all together, without having to talk about it beforehand. Maybe being in the gumball machine for however long they had been meant they knew one another well enough to know what they were thinking. For a second, Bobert was the only one in the courtyard not running in one direction or another. He couldn't help but think that they were leaving him out on purpose.

His mom's voice rang in his head, telling him to be kinder to himself. He felt a pang of worry that his parents must have gotten home before him, and that was when his instinct to run also kicked in.

Bobert wasn't a good climber, but he was close to a wall, and so that felt like a better idea than trying to run past the wizard and through the castle. Almost as soon as he started moving, though, he heard Matt sigh and mutter something. In an instant, his arms were still swinging at his sides but his legs refused to budge, like in one of those dreams where you try to run but can't, no matter how hard you try. He looked around and saw that everyone else was in the same situation.

Matt the Wizard started doing his evil chuckle/cough thing again, one arm stretched out, holding a wand. "Nice try!" he said, and the parrot on his shoulder squawked in agreement. "Actually, not a nice try at all! That hurt my feelings. I can't believe you thought I wouldn't be powerful enough or smart enough to keep you under a spell. Several, actually, because I am that good at wizarding!" He barked out another laugh, then did a little flourish with his wand. Now Bobert found his hand moving without him being able to do anything about it. He stared in horror as his palm turned to face him. Then a loud clap echoed throughout the courtyard as two hundred hands slapped two hundred foreheads at the same time.

"There's also a protective spell around the courtyard," Matt went on, "so don't try anything while I'm not looking. And because I'm so good at this magic stuff, there's one last spell on all the birds in the area, turning them into an alarm system. If anyone tries to leave, there'll be a whole lot of squawking going on. Right, Camila?" He looked at the parrot on his shoulder, who looked uninterested in squawking on command. Matt huffed, then waved his wand again, and Bobert felt his legs unstick. "Dinner will be coming soon, so I'm going to go get changed into my fancy robes. No more running away, or I'll make you smack yourselves even harder." With that he went back inside, and the courtyard got loud with chatter and movement. Bobert watched another few kids try to climb the wall again, but then their muscles seized up and they fell to the ground with a light thud.

Bobert waited for everyone else to go get a sleeping sack first. It was only fair for them to have the better options. They'd been sleeping inside a gumball machine, after all.

As they broke off into groups, he thought about Candelabra and Stanbert and Jennizabeth back in the plaza, suddenly panicked at the thought that he might lose all progress he had made throughout the day. Would they think that he'd left them by choice, that he didn't want to be friends anymore? Was it silly to be sadder about the fact that he was alone than the fact that he had been cursed?

When the line for the sleeping sacks subsided, Bobert stood up to go, hoping he'd still have a place to lay it down.

The only one left was torn at the bottom, so it wasn't actually a sack anymore, and it smelled a little mildewy, but it was soft on the inside and a cool maroon color, so Bobert brought it back to where he'd been sitting. Nearby, he noticed a spot next to the husky-voiced girl with the long braids, who was talking to the tall kid with the big bushy hair who'd been running around earlier.

He started setting up his bag, and hoped that they would bring him into their conversation. *What's your name, new kid?* he imagined the girl asking.

Except she didn't. Neither of them looked at him. It seemed he was right back where he'd started the day. If he ever made it back home, he was going to have a whole lot to catch his parents up on. He hoped he'd get to sooner rather than later.

Bobert had to comfort himself by listening to their conversation. He learned that the girl, Sylvinthia, had been stuck inside the machine for at least thirty years. She didn't know exactly how long, but she said that right before she got pulled into the gumball machine, someone had tried to block out the sun with a big rock, and that had happened when Bobert's parents were little. Jarrediah, the tall kid, blinked at her. "Wait, so you're actually a grown-up?"

"Do I look like a grown-up?" Sylvinthia asked, rolling her eyes. "A lot of us might be older than we look, technically. Obviously, time didn't move on inside the gumball machine." She sat cross-legged on her ratty sleep sack and started picking at the yellowing grass nearby. Bobert thought he saw a look of sadness pass over her features, but it was gone a second later.

"I guess not," Jarrediah said. Then he brightened up. "Which means maybe I'll keep growing! I was only inside for a couple of years, I think."

"Great," Sylvinthia said, tossing the grass she'd collected aside. "It'll make it even harder for our friends and family to recognize us." She bit her lip and looked at Bobert. "You were out in the world. Do you know if people were looking for us?"

Bobert swallowed hard and looked down at his feet, unable to think of a lie.

"Well, maybe *now* someone will come find us," Sylvinthia finished, sounding hopeful.

Bobert thought about his parents again, and how worried

they'd probably be after just an hour of not knowing where he was. He wondered if Candelabra and the others had told everyone by now. Maybe they would come and find him, now that it was clear the gumball machine really was cursed. And the rest of these kids could be saved too.

Bobert felt so bad for them that he wanted to hug them, but he didn't know if they'd want to be hugged. Instead he sat there, trying to comfort them by being quiet and nearby and hoping they'd all be rescued soon.

In town, Candelabra, Stanbert, and Jennizabeth stared at the empty space where the gumball machine used to be.

"That was weird," Stanbert said, flooded with relief that it was the machine that had disappeared and not Candelabra.

"What happened?" Jennizabeth said, putting a hand on Candelabra's shoulder as if checking to make sure she was still there.

"I'm not sure," Candelabra said, so softly her friends almost couldn't hear her.

She looked back down at her hand, which still held two nefickles and the mysterious eraser. The third nefickle was on the ground, where it had landed after a couple of bounces and a little roll. She had a feeling like she was standing in quicksand. Like the more she struggled, the further she sank.

Who could blame her for being certain right away that what

they were dealing with was an evil scheme? It was Nefaria, after all. When things felt off, a scheme was usually to blame. Last time she hadn't sensed it coming, and she wasn't going to let that happen again.

She clenched her fists by her side, as if she were hanging on to the world, begging it to stop doing whatever it was doing. "This is an evil scheme. I just know it."

"The machine is?" Jennizabeth asked.

"All of it. The machine. This eraser. I don't know how, exactly. But we have to tell someone."

Without waiting for Stanbert and Jennizabeth to respond, she started heading toward the adults on the other side of the plaza. Most of the adults were still busy yelling at one another, the way they always did after town-hall meetings, but a few seemed to notice the trio of kids heading their way.

"Gather the Elders!" Candelabra called out, as soon as she was close enough that they could hear her. She could see Stanbert's moms in the crowd, and Mr. Barracooties, the shoe repairman. Her parents didn't go to town halls anymore. They said they didn't agree with just putting the seven oldest people in Nefaria second in command after the king.

Jennizabeth and Stanbert were trying to calm Candelabra down, but mostly because it felt weird interrupting an Elder meeting. They knew Candelabra's whole thing about schemes, though—how determined she was to not fall for one again—so when she ignored them, they just followed her quietly.

"The Elders are inside," one of Stanbert's moms said. "But it's getting late and you know how they get about their bedtimes. What's this about, honey?"

"There's an evil scheme," she said. "The gumball machine. It disappeared. And I have the eraser for someone I don't know. I'm not sure what's happening, but I'm sure it's evil."

There was a silence in the air, and finally Principal Choochoo, who had been standing at the edge of the crowd, stepped forward. She was used to Candelabra ringing the alarm about evil schemes. "Why don't you start from the beginning?" she prompted.

Candelabra took a deep, impatient breath but did as she was told, covering as many details as she could remember. There were definitely gaps in her memory, but the important bits were there: they'd been daring one another to test the curse, the gumball machine had disappeared, and she had the eraser of someone she couldn't remember. When she was done, she immediately felt better. There, it was out. Now the adults would know what to do. They would save whoever Bobert was, and they'd figure out what had happened with the gumball machine. They would get to the bottom of this.

The relief she felt wasn't long-lived, though, because she could see the looks on the faces of the adults around them. And they seemed confused. Weren't adults supposed to know what to do? Weren't they supposed to understand what had happened? Weren't they at least supposed to pretend?

They were just looking around right now, some at one another, some at Candelabra, some across the plaza at where the machine had been. Some were arguing about where, exactly, that was. One guy in a vest argued that the machine hadn't been there for years. But he was wearing a vest, so no one really paid attention to him anyway. He was the village vest guy, and he only knew stuff about vests, nothing else.

"What are we going to do?" Candelabra asked. She was tired of everyone just thinking and muttering. She wanted action.

"We are not going to approve any more monkey business, that's what we're going to do!" Vest Guy shouted. "We've got the monkey dry cleaners, the monkey toy store, and now the Elders have approved the license for a monkey jewelry store? Too much monkey business! Too much monkey business!" He was clearly trying to get a chant going.

"I meant about Bobert. About the gumball machine."

The adults fell silent again. No one rushed to action, which made Candelabra want to scream.

"And who, exactly, is Bobert?" Principal Choochoo said, answering for the whole crowd, which was starting to slowly disperse, losing interest. Only the sensitive adults who knew Candelabra's history stayed behind. On the way out, someone rudely muttered that schemes were no big deal.

Candelabra groaned and opened her backpack. She rummaged through and pulled out the class portrait, but was distracted by two adults in the crowd. Even though she hadn't studied the portrait long, Candelabra could tell right away that they were somehow connected to this Bobert person. The woman had the same button nose as Bobert, the same grayish eyes. His dad, though probably much taller than Bobert, had the same brown floppy curls that were in the portrait, and they all shared the same olive skin.

And now Candelabra knew for sure, even if the adults couldn't see it. She ran up to the two adults, showing them the portrait. "This is your son, right? Bobert?"

She expected them to nod. To burst into tears and demand that something be done.

Instead they just looked at her with blank expressions. It was so obvious that he was their kid. Candelabra looked at the picture, just to make sure she wasn't imagining things. They looked at it too, but they didn't say no. They didn't say yes, either. It was as if they couldn't remember him. It was as if no one could.

SOMEHOW, Bobert managed to fall asleep.

Even though there were two hundred other bodies sleeping near him, tossing and turning, snoring, talking in their sleep (one kid sneezed in between snores!); even though the ground was hard beneath the grass; even though the sleep sack smelled like wet goat and the night air cooled down more than he would have expected; even though he was not at home in the comfort of his own bed, with his parents sleeping nearby, ready to protect him, help him, provide for him; even though he'd barely eaten any of the scorpion pizza that had arrived way too late in the night, cold and coagulated; Bobert did sleep. It had been a long, wild day.

He woke up to the brightness of a sun that had shot past the dawn and straight into full-fledged morning. There were a lot of voices, and he really had to pee.

He rubbed his eyes, confused just for the briefest of seconds as to where he was. Then he heard Matt's grating voice shouting out over the sounds of morning birds. "Armor on the left! Weapons in this line over here to the right! If your suit of armor is incomplete, please go to the back and see my cat, Justin. He is watching over the spare parts."

Bobert looked around for Sylvinthia or Jarrediah, but their sleeping bags were empty. He stood up, yawning, trying to rub the sleep from his eyes. Most of the other kids were making their way toward the front, near the castle. He felt a sharp disappointment that no one had come to rescue him during the night, but he felt a sharper need to pee, so he decided to deal with that first. The crowd of sleepy children had split off into three separate lines by the double doors Matt had burst out of last night. Matt had just told them about the left and the right lines, so he got in the middle line, figuring it was for an outhouse or maybe some breakfast, which would also be nice.

Almost as soon as he was standing in line, he felt a tug at his sleeve. He looked behind him and saw a little kid, maybe seven or eight years old. "Hey, mister," the boy said, his voice high-pitched and squeaky. "What are we doing here?"

Bobert shrugged as he answered. "I'm hoping this is the line for the bathroom."

The girl standing in front of him turned around, her auburn hair still mussed from sleep. "This is the line for helmets. The outhouse is that way, but some kid said the smell was so bad it

literally bit him, so we've been using those bushes over there."
She pointed toward the far end of the courtyard, where there
was apparently another line.

"So, what's happening?" Bobert asked the girl. He didn't
want to bother her, but not asking a question he wanted to
know the answer to felt too much like the Bobert from before.
True, it hadn't even been a whole day since "before." But
Bobert didn't want to go back to the Bobert who'd existed without Candelabra, Stanbert, and Jennizabeth. The Bobert who'd
existed without being seen. He didn't want that Bobert to exist
in whatever world this was.

"The dude's dressing us up or whatever," the girl said.
Bobert had never heard anyone under forty say the word 'dude'
before. It was a word that famously existed in all kingdoms; it
just hadn't been fashionable since Bobert's parents were kids.
"We're gonna get all suited up and stuff and be his army, I
guess."

"You guess," Bobert repeated, almost a question.

He looked around, wondering if any of the other gumball
kids were gonna try to run again. If they were going to try
anything again. He wondered how many ways they'd tried to
escape from that gumball machine, how many times they'd
tired their voices out screaming for help long before he arrived.

The girl shrugged and turned to the front again. Bobert
stepped out of line, feeling somehow responsible, feeling like he

had to do something. He sighed and headed toward the bathroom bushes. Whatever was going to happen next, he didn't want to have a full bladder for it.

It took almost an hour for all the kids to get armor and weapons (not to mention pee, get some water from a fountain at the front of the castle, and eat some breakfast gruel that Matt so generously provided).

Matt looked out at his army, with Camila the parrot perched on one shoulder, and Justin the cat perched on the other.

The sight wasn't quite what he'd been dreaming of when he came up with his scheme all those years ago. For one, they were all so short. And it had been really hard to find child-sized armor without raising suspicions. He'd had to scour garage sales and antique stores in every corner of the kingdom. So most of the suits he'd bought weren't complete—they were missing an elbow here, a knee there, a whole torso sometimes. He'd given them a little magical spit shine, but there was still rust on a lot of the armor.

And the weapons. Oh boy, the weapons. Most of these kids couldn't hold a sword with two hands, much less one. There was the constant clang of steel hitting his precious courtyard stones. One girl was trying to pull at the bow and arrow she'd chosen for herself, and accidentally sent an arrow shooting straight up in the air. "Watch it," Matt yelled. "You're going to poke someone's eye out."

Camila shifted on his shoulder, and Matt could feel her wanting to comment on the situation. "Oh, just say it," he said.

"What?" Camila squawked. "I wasn't going to say anything."

"They're a little rough around the edges," Matt admitted. "But I'll get them in shape, no problem. Once I get the attack spell going, they'll look much better." He watched as one kid—he couldn't have been older than seven—tried to put a helmet on but lost his balance and fell over onto his back. He struggled there, like an overturned turtle, screaming for help. "Plus, it only helps with the plan if they look helpless. No knight is going to try to fight back."

"Before anyone can fight back, there has to be someone capable of starting the fight," Camila said, ruffling her feathers. "Don't you think they should at least be able to walk to the royal castle?"

"Shut up, bird," Matt said.

He took a deep breath, trying to picture this ending with him getting a parade from his loving and loyal subjects. When he failed to picture it, he raised his hands up to ask for quiet in the courtyard. Except everyone just continued clanging in their oversized armor and talking among themselves. Matt cleared his throat as loudly as he could. Still nothing.

So, he groaned and pulled out his wand from inside his robes. "Roth karoth ploipity plop!"

Silence fell over the courtyard. Matt the Evil Wizard smirked. He still had it. Some of the kids kept moving their mouths, not realizing that they were no longer making sounds. Eventually, though, they all figured it out and looked toward him.

"It's a good day, children. Today we take over Nefaria." He waved the wand again. "Plooose papoose, move your caboose."

It was a classic spell, meant to control someone else's body, which all wizards learn when they're young. Not in school, but mostly from their parents, who use it all the time when trying to keep their rambunctious wizard toddlers from running into traffic or knocking over an orange display at the fruit vendor's.

It was a little tricky to achieve with two hundred kids at once, but it helped that they were kids, and much more susceptible to magic. He was going to have them march in unison, let the clatter of the armor and the drumbeat of their footsteps announce Nefaria's doom. A new reign of wizard rule was about to begin!

And the spell did, technically, work. The kids *tried* to get into the formation that Matt was wishing them into. Twenty across and ten deep, a big rectangular battalion to show his manpower. Or childpower. However, the kids weren't used to marching, and definitely not in armor.

Bobert—who was wearing less of a knight's armor, and more like discarded pieces of metal shaped into parts that kind of fit on his body—had to use his arms to lift his legs in order to move, they were so heavy.

Another kid tried to move too quickly and tipped over, falling directly into a line of kids who had managed to get in formation, and knocking them down like dominoes. There was a terrific series of screams and metal clangs as kids fell onto one another, and others tried to run away from the mayhem.

Matt sighed and put a hand to his forehead. "This might take longer than I thought it would."

"You could always have them take off the armor?" Camila suggested.

"An army without armor? Don't be ridiculous," Matt scoffed. "No one would be afraid. It would look like a field trip. I just need to work on the spells a little, have them practice."

For the next hour or so, Matt just tried to get the group into formation. He finally got it to look like more or less what he wanted it to, but when he had them take a single step forward, there was another domino effect and nearly all the kids ended up on the ground.

Bobert was one of them. His suit didn't allow for a lot of movement in the knee area, and so he had toppled over, barely letting go of his oversized sword in time to catch himself with his hands. Now he was trying to push himself off the ground and stand back up, but the armor weighed too much, and he was stuck facedown, trying to wriggle over, all the while hoping that if someone was going to come rescue him, it didn't happen at that exact moment, but a little later, when he wasn't in such an embarrassing position.

And if no one was going to come, which he had to admit seemed more and more likely, then it was clearly up to him to do something. How could he do that if he was stuck in his armor? He didn't know how he could do that even if he was standing upright.

He was already sweaty and tired, but Bobert felt a swell of energy go through him. These kids depended on him! Even if they couldn't see him, and even if he couldn't see how he was going to get them all out of this.

Just like he did when pushing through a final hill on the way back home, he grunted and managed to push off the ground into a sitting position. He wanted to pump his fist as a celebration, but his arm was too heavy to lift. Instead he looked over to the wizard, who was tugging at his beard.

"Curses!" Matt yelled.

"I think we're gonna need help," Camila squawked.

"Yes, I think you're right," he relented, looking out at the hopeless army he had built.

"Want me to fly over to the bookstore and get some army training manuals?"

"We don't have time for books!" Matt bellowed, his hat falling off his head from the force of it. He bent over to snatch it back up. "You watch over them. I'm going to Mount Tuku."

The bird cawed loudly, looking at Matt in disbelief. "You really think the greatest living warrior in Nefaria would help us?"

"For the right price, yes." Matt gathered his robes about him, brushing off some of the dirt on them. "Maybe I should change," he muttered to himself. "I'll set up some extra spells on my way out, but if anything goes wrong, send word to me with one of the hawks."

"The hawks try to eat me."

"With a hummingbird, then."

"Hummingbirds can't get all the way to Mount Tuku. They're fast, sure, but almost no range."

"Just send word, stupid bird!" Matt screamed.

Bobert watched Matt storm off, back into the castle. He had been at the very front of the formation, so he'd heard every word of Matt's exchange with Camila. He looked around, trying to see if anyone else had heard that Matt was leaving, but it looked like everyone was too busy trying to pick themselves back up from their latest fall, and tending to the little scrapes and bruises they'd gotten when they fell.

Bobert rolled himself over to the steps that led into the castle, and he used them to help lift himself onto his knees. He couldn't believe what he'd just heard. Was Matt really going to see Imogene Petunias? And would she really help an evil wizard take over the kingdom?

Bobert wanted to think that no, she wouldn't. After all, she wasn't a mercenary. She had earned the title of greatest warrior in Nefaria by being loyal to the king's army throughout her exploits. Still, Bobert was immediately excited at the thought that he might meet her! And maybe even be trained by her. How cool!

Well, kinda.

He tried to calm himself down. There was no way Imogene Petunias would listen to anything Matt had to say, much less agree to train his army.

But now that the famed warrior was on his mind, he started thinking about what she would do if she were in his situation. He pictured being forced to fight against his family, against his classmates, against all the people in Nefaria who were always so vigilant about evil schemes.

Imogene would never let it come to that.

Maybe this was another chance for him to break his own personal curse of invisibility. Maybe if he could get the other kids out of this, if he could help save Nefaria from being ruled by this weirdo wizard, then he would finally be as seen as he wanted to be.

Bravery did that to people: made them see you. Just look at Imogene Petunias. She was one of the most recognizable names and faces in Nefaria for a reason.

Sitting on the steps now, Bobert took off some of his armor, pretty sure that Camila and the old, sleepy cat in the back wouldn't care much while Matt was gone. He knew this might be the kids' only chance to escape before Matt could make them fight. That *he* might be the only chance they had.

He had to find a way to stop Matt's plan and save Nefaria. But how?

THE SECOND TOWN HALL MEETING had been going for an hour, though the adults hadn't really gotten anywhere. Stanbert was sleeping, curled under some chairs in the back. Candelabra was the only other kid there, most of her limbs jittering as she watched the adults discuss what to do. Jennizabeth had to go home when it got dark, though Candelabra suspected that she was mostly running away from the uncomfortable situation. Jennizabeth did that often, which was okay. Not everyone faced discomfort the same way.

The people who were clearly Bobert's parents had no memory of having a son, and in fact no one present could identify the kid in the class portrait. They were going off just Candelabra's testimony, which would have been easy to dismiss, if it weren't for Nefaria's evil-scheme protocol, which made it necessary to investigate every claim.

The adults kept getting distracted, though. Somehow, Vest

Guy was still trying to make this about the number of business licenses that the village had handed out to monkey entrepreneurs. Thankfully, it seemed that the rest of the adults were as sick of that guy as Candelabra was.

"The point is," Elder Gusbus said, "that there are too many unknowns. We can't go knocking on the door of every evildoer in the kingdom—that would take forever! Plus, we've thoroughly investigated the gumball-machine claims in the past, and nothing has ever come of it."

"Well, investigate again!" Candelabra said forcefully. "Round up some of the usual suspects. If we just sit back and don't do anything about it, we're asking for trouble. You remember what happened last time, right?"

Elder Gusbus sighed deeply, then whispered something to Elder Vanillabean sitting next to him. They conferred for a while before he finally leaned forward in his seat and spoke again, his voice gravelly from a long night (and life) of talking. "Very well, miss. We will convene a committee to decide the best course of action for investigating the gumball machine and its disappearance."

"And Bobert's!"

"Yes, another committee for that, too."

Everyone groaned. The Elders loved forming committees, which were mostly just comprised of different combinations of Elders. But that was how it had always been done. Elder

Gusbus slammed his hammer down, and it was decided.

The room began to empty. Candelabra stayed put, and so did Bobert's (likely) parents, who were talking to a few other adults. Bobert's maybe mom turned to look over her shoulder and saw Candelabra sitting there, and she stepped over.

"Shouldn't you be heading home?"

Candelabra shook her head. She couldn't find any words to say. Actually, the words were there. They were just stuck behind a big old lump of tears, and they weren't gonna come without the tears spilling out first. What if it was all her fault? Again.

Bobert's maybe mom took a seat next to her. She pulled out a bag of almonds and offered some to Candelabra.

"Thanks," Candelabra said, grabbing a handful. Eating helped. Plus, the almonds were seasoned with lime leaf and chili pepper, which was one of Candelabra's favorite combinations. She realized she hadn't eaten in way too long.

"Do your parents know where you are?"

Candelabra hesitated. "My sister does. She takes care of me." It was always strange bringing that up with people who didn't know. Especially because of where her sister was now, and how people reacted when they found out. It only drove the guilt deeper when people thought she couldn't take care of herself.

Her sister might worry if Candelabra didn't check in, it

was true. Thankfully, one of the spider monkeys that was at the town hall earlier was her neighbor and checked in on her often, and she had asked him to pass the message along to Sandraliere. "I don't want to wait for a committee," she said. "I want to go find him."

Bobert's maybe mom sighed, and she grabbed a handful of almonds for herself. "Okay, then, let's go looking. Billiam and I would like to help, if you're okay with that, and if your sister says it's okay."

Candelabra nodded eagerly. "You believe me, right?"

The woman didn't answer right away, looking down at the almonds and picking through them. She chewed, and her mind looked very far away. "Nefaria's a strange place to live, isn't it?"

Candelabra had never thought of it that way. She wondered if what had happened would have happened in another kingdom. Maybe in Infamia, or Los Angsteles. Definitely not in Jovialla. "Yeah," she said.

Bobert's maybe mom smiled at Candelabra, then stood up, brushing almond residue off her lap. "We'll start looking for him tomorrow. Go get some sleep."

Candelabra did as she was told, walking home through town, playing with Bobert's eraser. She thought about him throughout the night, and of every nook and cranny in the town and its surrounding mountains where someone could hide a gumball machine, or a child, or a bunch of children.

A part of her wondered if she was imagining everything. But it had only been a year since she'd put others in danger because of an evil scheme. She had been reckless, unvigilant. And to this day, she was dealing with the consequences. She always would.

So, no. Even though the evidence was flimsy, she wasn't going to let it happen again. If someone could stand between an evil scheme and this Bobert, even if she didn't know him at all, she would make sure someone was there. Even if it had to be her.

10

IMOGENE PETUNIAS poured herself a cup of coffee, cut herself a slice of pie, and walked out into the brisk morning to do what she loved best: put her feet up on the banister of her front deck and look out at the mountains. They were still shrouded in morning fog, and the air was still, as if it, too, were just waking up.

It would soon be too hot, but Imogene placed another log in the fire pit beside the lone chair on her deck. Her day would be spent up here, looking over the kingdom she'd helped protect and fought for so many times. Not that she particularly loved Nefaria. Imogene had the sense that she would have equally loved any land she was born into. But Imogene loved to fight. She was good at it. And all her battles had earned her this: the peace and quiet of a perfect view, a strong cup of coffee, the joy of making a fire whenever she pleased.

And, of course, pie.

She tried not to get her hopes up. After all, it wasn't Grandma

Gertrude's pie. But that was part of the joy of retirement: she was free to keep searching for a pie as good as Gertrude's.

She picked up the book she'd set down on the table beside her, but only made it as far as opening it and resting it on her stomach. Not yet, she thought. There was no rush. She sat forward to pull her sweater off, relishing the feeling of both the fresh air and the heat of the flames on her muscular arms.

She took another sip of her coffee, pushed her fork into the pie, and closed her eyes as she chewed. Good flavor to the crust, though not ideal flakiness. The filling had a pleasant taste, but a touch too sweet, and not spiced enough. It was satisfying, but it was no Grandma Gertrude's. That was okay. She had an icebox full of pies from all over the kingdom and would try another one after lunch.

She was about to take another bite when she heard footsteps on dewy grass, heavy panting. She put her pie down, grabbed the dagger hidden in her boot, and put it in her lap beneath the book, just in case. Whoever it was would be no match for Imogene in a fight, but the knife would also come in handy if the person merely annoyed her so much that she wanted to throw it at them.

"Yoo-hoo!" came a bellowing voice from over the hill.

All she saw at first was a pointy blue hat. Great. A wizard. They were always so chatty. She almost would have preferred if it had been a ghost. Even a ghost of someone she had killed in battle who was coming back to haunt her. A few moments later the wizard was below her deck, squinting up at her against the morning sun poking out from the mountain behind her.

"Hello there! I do not mean to disturb you, but I am here to request your services."

"I'm retired," Imogene spat back.

"Yes, Your Mightiness, I had heard. However, allow me to introduce myself. I am none other than the Great and Evil Wizard Matt; Purveyor of Wicked Wands; Chillest Wizard, Master of Blizzards; the Once and Future Cat Lord; Perpetrator of the Great Tickle Heist . . ."

Oh god, Imogene thought. He was going to carry on. "I'm not interested. Now get off my property or I'll show you off myself."

"I'm willing to pay," the wizard said.

Now he was really ruining her morning. Imogene stood from her chair, grabbing hold of the book and keeping the dagger hidden behind it. She wasn't the biggest or the tallest person, even off the battlefield, but she still had a way of standing that made others feel small. "Usually, when a person is retired," she said, speaking slowly and forcefully, hoping that her tone made it clear how stupid she thought the wizard was, "that means they are willing to not get paid anymore, in order to do nothing. You are interrupting my nothing-doing. Anyway, I was never in the business of renting out my fighting to just anyone with a coin purse."

"I didn't say *what* I was going to pay." The wizard had a big grin on his face as he said this.

"Last chance before I march down there and roll you back down the hill," Imogene said.

"Very well," the wizard said, and he started turning around, but then pretended like he'd just remembered something. "Unless you're interested in the recipe, that is."

Imogene narrowed her eyes. "What recipe?"

Now Matt put on a coy air, and Imogene cursed silently that she'd let the power shift toward this doofus. He held his smile for a little longer, no doubt savoring the look on her face. "Grandma Gertrude's apple pie."

Imogene gripped the deck banister to steady herself. "It's been lost."

"Has it, now?" Matt said. "Very well, then, off I go." He shrugged and turned, then started skipping away in the direction he came.

"Wait!" she shouted.

Matt turned back toward her. "You're interested in the recipe?"

She hated that he knew. She hadn't necessarily kept it quiet. That part of her agreement with the king had been no secret:

if the recipe was ever discovered, Imogene would be given it as a reward.

"Why do you have it?"

"Why does it matter? You're retired. I'll find someone else."

Imogene thought about threatening to strangle the recipe out of him. But instead, she was surprised that the only word she could say was "Please!"

Matt had reached inside his robes now and pulled out his wand, but instead of flourishing it, he cleared his throat. "Since I am coming to you with a request, I will be kind enough to explain the story—as long as you agree to the job I came here to offer you. The recipe is the pay; the story I'll throw in as a bonus."

"Why should I believe you?" Imogene asked. Her hand was squeezing the banister so hard she was getting splinters.

Now Matt gave his biggest smile. But then he waved his wand in the air and muttered what sounded like gibberish. As soon as he was done, there was a *ding!* like the sound of a toaster oven, and a slice of pie was floating in front of Imogene.

It was absolutely beautiful. Perfect tendrils of steam rose from its golden filling, and the buttery crust shone in the morning light.

Imogene had only had the pleasure of eating the famous apple pie twice, as a little girl, long before she was a warrior. But in her memory the pie was perfectly clear.

She reached out to the floating pie in front of her, not bothering to search for a plate or a fork. She broke off the front tip of the slice. More steam billowed out, the roasted apples inside golden brown and fragrant. It looked like the pie. It smelled like it too. She brought it to her mouth and plopped it in, not bothering to let it cool.

This was pie you had to close your eyes to truly eat. You had to experience the pie, and the pie only. This was Grandma Gertrude's pie.

She looked down at the doofus below. "How do I know this isn't just magic? How do I know it's real?"

"Oh, come on," Matt said with a scoff. "Everyone knows that wizards can't conjure up food unless they have the recipe for it. That's stuff you learn in middle school."

Imogene had never made it to middle school. But she was too full of the pie's warmth (in more ways than one) to get truly angry over the reminder. She reached for another piece. "What's the job?"

"I need you to train my army. They're, uh . . ." He trailed off, gesturing with his hand as he tried to find the right word. "Inexperienced."

Imogene looked back at her deck. The fire was still burning, and her coffee was losing its steam, but there was more inside. The vision she'd had for her day could still come true. And she could probably eat the rest of the floating pie, really savor it.

But then tomorrow it would be gone, and the day after that, too. She'd believed she'd never be able to eat this pie again. Now she had a chance to eat it as many times as she wanted.

"Do I want to know why you need the army?"

"Does it matter?"

Imogene ate another little piece. She was taken back to the past, to her time on the road with her uncle, to all those moments of hope she'd had over the years, throughout the kingdom, wishing to somehow stumble into someone who had the recipe. She'd eaten so many pies, probably every pie available for sale in the kingdom, and a lot of homemade ones too, and nothing had ever come close to this. "Two weeks, that's all you get."

Matt grinned, then nodded.

"I'll go pack my bags."

11

MATT HAD LEFT DAYS AGO, and the courtyard had the feel of a classroom where the teacher stepped out for a minute but hasn't come back in more than five. Normally, if that situation arose, Bobert would be sitting quietly. And, sure, some other kids were doing so, looking lost without instructions. Some others were trying to get the hang of marching in their armor, which maybe was the right thing to do.

Bobert, though, had made up his mind. He was going to find a way to save them.

He began by taking in every detail about his surroundings that he could. He watched as kids tried to scale the wall around the courtyard to escape, but if they managed to dig their fingers into the nooks and crannies of the stone wall, the spell Matt had cast on the area shoved them back down as soon as they got to the top. As for Matt's accomplices, two girls had taken to holding a miserable Justin the cat and petting him way too aggressively while Camila laughed nearby like an underpaid substitute teacher.

With his new mission, Bobert actually didn't mind his perpetual invisibility, which allowed him to move around the courtyard unbothered. And while trying to find escape routes for them, Bobert had discovered that the spells Matt had cast meant that the castle had very specific areas it would let the kids into. He would have thought the castle was completely off-limits, but that wasn't the case. He was able to go into the kitchen, where the icebox was available (no mustard, though). When he tried to go into the pantry, however, he could open the door but not enter. Which was a shame, because there was some mustard in there, just out of reach. The basement bathroom was fair game, but the whole upstairs part of the castle was magically blocked off. Bobert had tried, but some invisible barrier blocked him as soon as he tried stepping onto the stairwell. He tried to warn a boy in overalls with pigtails who was running in a full sprint toward the stairs, but the boy couldn't hear Bobert, or ignored him, and he bounced off the barrier in a way that looked both painful and a little fun.

Sure, Bobert was still lonely. And he still pretended to be a part of the groups around him while he explored the castle looking for anything that could help them.

Sometimes Bobert caught parts of conversations between

the other kids and wondered why none of them were talking about their hopes of being rescued. But they'd been in the gumball machine for who knows how long without anyone coming for them.

They were used to being forgotten, Bobert realized.

He wondered if he should tell them about who Imogene Petunias was, but he wasn't sure they would want another reminder that the world had continued on without them.

Another curious thing happened as he listened to the gumball kids and thought about saving them: he learned about them. Learned how long some of them had been gone for, learned which of them were picky eaters, and which of them had missed the outdoors so much they actually seemed happy to be at the castle (most of them, but Sylvinthia more than anyone).

"What if we convince the parrot to talk the wizard out of it?" the tall boy named Jarrediah asked. He spoke often about his two annoying sisters, but the way he complained made Bobert think he really missed them.

The group had been sitting in a circle near Bobert for hours now, suggesting ways to get out of the castle. But, like the girl Bobert had talked to in line, they didn't really seem all that motivated. It was more like they were just passing the time.

"How would we do that?" Javitopher mumbled. He was

holding his face up with his palms while leaning his elbows on his knee, looking like a combination of bored and hopeless.

"We can bribe her," Jarrediah suggested. Bobert didn't think that was a great idea, but he wasn't particularly good at shooting down other people's ideas. Or at interrupting conversations he was eavesdropping on.

"With what?" Sylvinthia asked. She was a little more comfortable shooting down ideas that didn't fit in with her strong sense of logic. "We don't have anything."

"Okay, then we don't bribe her," Jarrediah said. "We can just convince her with our words." He snapped his fingers, like an idea had just occurred to him and he had to announce it somehow. "I bet the wizard isn't, like, the best pet owner. One of us could promise to take her home if she lets us go!"

"I have a bunch of snakes at home. They'd probably eat her," Javitopher mumbled. "At least, I think I still have them. How long do snakes live?"

"We don't really know if she's the wizard's pet," Sylvinthia pointed out. "It seems like she could just fly away if she wanted to." They all turned to look at Camila, who was perched on the branch of a tree poking over the courtyard wall. She cocked her head at the group, as if she could hear what they were saying.

A moment went by as they all thought some more. Bobert took another bite of the tomato-and-grass sandwich that the kids had been forced to make themselves for lunch every day since Matt the Wizard had left. The tomatoes themselves were actually pretty good, but the sandwiches were pretty bad. They needed some mustard or hot sauce or *something*.

Suddenly, remembering his earlier exploration of the castle, Bobert had an idea.

He wasn't technically sitting in the circle with the others, but he tried to angle his body toward the others so that maybe they would notice and include him.

Then he thought about what he had learned from his last day before getting cursed, which was probably the best day he had had in a long time. What had he done differently? The only thing he could think of was this: he'd been brave. He had been willing to come with them to the gumball machine, and willing to be the one to use it. People liked others who were brave.

He cleared his throat, ready to speak up. Then Sylvinthia made eye contact with him and he looked away, swinging his legs in the other direction. Why? Why did his body do this? Why did it rebel against his brain's wishes? Why did it agree to its invisibility?

"New kid. You have an idea?"

His pulse quickened, and even though he knew it was silly, he pointed at himself. "Me?"

"Yeah. It looked like you were going to say something."

Emboldened by being visible for the first time since Matt

had pointed at him when they'd all shown up, Bobert cleared his throat and licked his lips. To escape this place, these kids needed him to be brave. To speak up.

"Well," he started, unsure of himself now that he had to say his idea out loud. "We've been trying to think about how to get out of being in his army once he's back and he makes us march," he said, as if he'd been part of the group the whole time. "But maybe we've been thinking about it all wrong. What if we just don't let him *in*?"

The others stared at Bobert. Surely he'd said something incredibly not-smart, and for that he was going to become invisible.

What the others were actually doing, though, was waiting for the flaw in his plan to make itself clear. Because none of them could find one right away. They looked at Sylvinthia to double-check. "He might be able to cast a spell once he's back to undo everything," she said, "but it's worth a shot."

"How do we keep him from coming into his own castle, though?"

They all immediately looked around for ideas. Bobert tried to remember what big heavy furniture there was inside the castle that they could move in front of the doors. Or maybe some rope to tie the doors together. But he couldn't be sure. He had been exploring ways to get out, not ways to keep other people out. Looking around the courtyard offered no other ideas.

"We could just use our bodies, right?" Jarrediah said. "There's two hundred of us and just one of him."

"That's a good backup plan," Sylvinthia said. "But remember, he has us all under his spell. He might be able to easily move us out of the way. It'd be better if we used objects."

"I think he went to get help," Bobert said. "Like, a warrior to train us."

"Maybe we should split up," Javitopher said, his head finally out of his hands so they could understand him. "It's a big castle."

"I've seen bigger," Jarrediah said.

Bobert's heart sank the slightest bit at the idea of splitting up, just when he was part of a group again. He was used to being alone, sure. But just because we get used to something doesn't mean that's how we prefer it. He wondered what Candelabra was doing, what the whole town was doing. Maybe there was already a search party looking for them. Judging by the mountains, they weren't that far from town. He was sure his parents were doing whatever they could to track him down. Bobert wondered about the other kids' parents. Where were they? How come two hundred kids had remained missing this whole time, without anyone making a big fuss? The thought made him want to go to the Council of Elders and yell at them, made him want to search all of Nefaria for people in harm's way. But more than that, it made him want to start on the plan right away.

"Good idea," Sylvinthia said. "New kid and I will take the inside; you two explore out here. Try to spread the word, too. If this is gonna work, we need everyone to be in on the plan. Or at least as many people as possible."

Bobert couldn't help but smile at the fact that Sylvinthia wanted to team up with him, even if it was just to help look for something to barricade themselves in the castle with. It felt good to be picked.

They had tried everything and everywhere and everyone.

Candelabra had joined Bobert's presumed parents for the last two days, going around to every castle, compound, and lair that was known to be evil, or had the potential of evilness. (Sometimes there were flags announcing it, and sometimes you could tell just by looking at a place.) Despite not having any memories of Bobert, the parents had a whole room in their house where an eleven-year-old clearly lived, so they felt a certain sadness, even if not too deeply. The nature of Nefaria and its schemes meant people often had rooms in their homes that they didn't fully understand. Rooms inhabited by ghosts or memories or a bunch of snakes.

"Your sister didn't want to come with us?" they asked at one point.

Candelabra just shook her head, not wanting them to worry

about anything other than Bobert. The committee the Elders had convened was still deciding the best approach and setting rules and procedures, and until they had the full authority of the kingdom behind them, it was up to them to search.

They invoked a Nefarian law that allowed common people to search potentially evil homes and businesses, but so far they had found no trace of either Bobert or the gumball machine. They *had* discovered a pit of alligators that had lasers strapped to their heads and were practicing martial arts at Viscount Gary's mansion. But even Candelabra would admit that was pretty normal. If you went around knocking on everyone's door, you were bound to discover some scheme of some sort. That didn't mean it was necessarily evil. Candelabra knew of at least three friends who had martial arts–practicing reptiles at their homes.

Candelabra and Bobert's parents simply made a note to tell the committee later, then moved on to have lunch and talk about their options They'd strayed pretty far from town, into a neighboring village. It was weird to Candelabra how casual everyone was acting, as if everything was normal. She supposed they didn't know Bobert, which made it easier. Of course, she didn't know Bobert either.

It was sad, really, how Nefarians just accepted the way things were. Candelabra sometimes wondered if they no longer felt a sense of injustice, no longer could bring themselves to care about others' suffering.

She moved around the potatoes on her plate. They were at a roadside restaurant, everyone exhausted from the days of searching, and mostly from the failure of those searches.

"Where are we going next?" Candelabra asked, dropping her fork with a sigh.

Bobert's parents looked at each other, then at Candelabra. His mom reached out her hand and put it on top of hers. Not a good sign. "Honey, we were thinking it's time for us to rest. You should go home, unwind a little with your sister."

Candelabra pulled her hand away. "What? No!" She turned to Bobert's parents. "If you want to keep looking without me, that's okay. But I'm not going to stop looking until we find him." She grabbed at her fork and stabbed two potato chunks, then shoved them into her mouth as if to help make her point.

Bobert's dad smiled, and made his voice soft. "That's very sweet. We really appreciate your efforts, and your passion. It means the world to us, and it would mean the world to Bobert, I'm sure. But the truth is, we don't even know if he's out there. We don't know for sure there is a scheme happening."

Candelabra was still chewing the potatoes, but she couldn't help but spit out, "No! Of course there's a scheme! You have a son."

Bobert's mom wiped at some of the potato bits that had hit her in the face. "We don't know that. The room in our house might just be for our nephew. He visits us a lot." She sighed, maybe responding to the anger Candelabra felt reddening her face. "We're going to keep looking, of course. You should keep talking to friends about it at school. Keep thinking about where else to look. But right now we could all use some rest."

"But we still haven't looked at . . ." Inside the quicksand pits, at the spider-monkey gym, at Dr. Prettybad's goat farm? But they'd looked at all of those places, and had come away with nothing. She felt tears welling up in her eyes again. The door of the restaurant opened then, and Candelabra used it as an excuse to fix her eyes elsewhere.

Two people came in. A wizard in dirty blue robes, red-cheeked and sweaty, and a fit and strong-looking woman who immediately seemed familiar to Candelabra. She watched the odd couple cross the restaurant and take a seat a few tables away, by the window. The wizard removed his hat and put it on the table, and Candelabra could hear the woman saying, "Take that dirty thing off the table before I throw it out the window."

The wizard quickly moved it and put it on his lap instead. At Candelabra's table, the adults resumed eating, Bobert's mom giving her hand one last pat, taking her silence as acceptance of the new plan to split up. Candelabra kept watching the other table.

"Why does that woman look familiar?" Candelabra said.

Now the human temptation to stare, especially when someone has called attention to a person, took over the whole table.

"Oh my god!" Bobert's mom said quietly.

"Is that who I think it is?" Bobert's dad whispered.

"What, who is it?"

"Imogene Petunias," Bobert's mom said, hunching closer to the table so that the famed warrior wouldn't hear her getting starstruck. Now Candelabra recognized her from her textbooks, and from various programs she'd watched on her wizard screen at home. Wow! Nefaria's greatest living warrior, at the same restaurant as her!

"What's she doing here?" Candelabra asked.

"And who is that man with her?"

They all tried to watch as nonchalantly as possible, but it felt like a fun little distraction from the worries they all had been dealing with for the last few days. The server approached the table by the window, and it was clear that she also recognized Imogene Petunias. She immediately became flustered.

"Oh wow, I'm such a huge fan!" she exclaimed.

The wizard, however, responded, "Ah, yes, you're aware of my work? Well, I'll gladly sign your paper or whatever you have there. Or I can use my wand and cast a spell on you, if you like?

What would you prefer? My signature tattooed on your skin? A third arm? How about dolphin flippers?"

Candelabra cringed. It seemed like everyone but him knew what the server was going to say next. "Um, no, thank you. I was—"

"Hey, don't knock dolphin flippers. I know we're a land-locked kingdom, but they come in very handy in rivers and lakes. Even in the tub. Makes bath time much more fun." The wizard was now trying to grab the paper, which was clearly just the notepad she used to take down people's orders.

"I was talking to *her*!" the server said, pulling away from his grip. She turned to Imogene. "It's an honor having you here," she said. "Do you mind if I have my portrait taken with you?"

Imogene shot a smug grin at Matt, then smiled at the server. "Sure, that would be fine. How's your apple pie?"

The server took their order, then pulled up a chair next to Imogene so that the manager could come by and paint their portrait together.

"Wait," Bobert's dad said, wiping his mouth with his napkin and setting his fork and knife on his plate to signal he was done. "I recognize that guy. He lives near town." He started snapping his fingers, a weird thing adults did to try to remember stuff. Candelabra had never done that, and she hoped she never would. "I know! Isn't he the guy who tried to capture the king in a haunted house a few years ago?"

"Oh yeah," Bobert's mom said, also doing that weird snapping thing. "And it wasn't even haunted by real ghosts or anything; it was just a fake haunted house like the kind they have at amusement parks and in parking lots during Spooky Month."

"Wait," Candelabra said. "That sounds evil."

"Sure," Bobert's dad said. "Cockamamie, but evil. At least it was trying to be."

"Why haven't we checked out his castle, then?"

The adults chuckled. "That guy?" Bobert's dad said. "No, I don't think so. He doesn't quite have the . . . skills to pull off a curse and a disappearance."

"But he's hanging out with the greatest living warrior in Nefaria. Maybe he's connected. Like, with more evil guys or something. Maybe it's a big project and not just one person."

The adults were back to eating, just occasionally glancing at the odd couple across the restaurant. "Big conspiracies like that are hard to keep quiet, honey," Bobert's mom explained. "The simpler explanation here is that they knew each other from school or something."

"He's like a million years old."

"Well, maybe he's her uncle." Bobert's mom moved a hand to cup Candelabra's cheek. It was a gesture that Candelabra was used to getting from adults, and usually it succeeded in comforting her. Right now, though, it felt like just a nice way to tell her to be quiet.

Candelabra shoved some more potatoes into her mouth, chewing without any appetite, unable to ignore Imogene and the wizard. Something didn't feel right to her, and if the adults at the table weren't gonna listen, then it was up to her to figure out what was going on.

12

BOBERT AND SYLVINTHIA tried to walk nonchalantly toward the front of the castle. Bobert had heard Matt tell the parrot to notify him if anything went wrong, so while it felt very much like the bird didn't care what the kids were doing, they figured it was better not to raise any suspicions.

Bobert began to casually whistle until Sylvinthia pointed out that the only people who whistled were jolly old men and people about to do something borderline evil.

"Right," Bobert said. "Sorry."

They made it to the big front doors and pushed them open, as if they were just going to the bathroom. Bobert found himself wanting to go toward the basement, but Sylvinthia tiptoed her way straight ahead, toward the great hall that stretched before them.

It wasn't that great a hall. The lighting was really bad, and instead of cool portraits of ancestors or whatever, there were just three off-kilter portraits of Matt giving finger guns. In all three of them!

"I can't believe we've been captured by such a dork of a wizard," Bobert said. Part of him felt a little mean saying it. The truth was that Bobert felt a little sad for Matt, since there weren't pictures of anyone else on the wall. But it felt like he had to be a little mean toward their captor, if only to make conversation with Sylvinthia.

It worked. Sylvinthia laughed out loud, then tried to shush him, though it felt like she was just shushing herself.

The end of the hall opened up to a den of sorts, next to a dining room. "We can probably use that table," Sylvinthia said. "It'll take a lot of us to push it to the main entrance, but there *are* a lot of us."

Bobert approached the table, which was extremely long but had only four chairs, one on each side. He ran a finger over the top, and a big cloud of dust puffed up and made him cough. He rubbed the finger on his pants. "Ew."

"He has such bad taste," Sylvinthia muttered, staring at a zebra-print couch with leopard-print throw pillows on it.

Bobert had just been thinking that he liked the couch and was glad he hadn't commented on it. If he had, would Sylvinthia start ignoring him? Could *he* someday turn evil because he liked zebra-print couches?

No, that was silly. He was going to help everyone get rescued. That was the exact opposite of evil.

He turned to Sylvinthia as he absent-mindedly flicked a lamp on and off. "What's the first thing you want to do when we're free?"

Sylvinthia was quiet for a while, picking up pillows on the couch and fluffing them, then coughing when clouds of dust shot up. "Let's just take it one step at a time," she said. "You?"

"I haven't really thought about it yet," he answered, though he had. Of course he had. He just thought that his answer was even sadder than Matt's wall of self-portraits.

They continued exploring. They couldn't go into the bedrooms that were to the left of the den, because of whatever spell Matt had put on them. So they backtracked to the dining room and made their way into the kitchen. Remembering a graphic novel he had read about ninja chefs, Bobert grabbed some wooden cooking utensils, figuring that maybe they could slip them in the door handles and keep them from opening that way. Sylvinthia grabbed a chef's knife, but then left it behind when she realized that it was so dull it wouldn't be able to cut through butter.

"We could use all the swords and axes and stuff too," Sylvinthia said. "That might be enough. But we should make sure we have all the doors covered."

They tried the pantry again, just in case they could get some better condiments for dinner, but it was still under a spell. On their way out of the kitchen they grabbed a couple of cookies from the counter; then they went through another hall, this one even less great. There were bats hanging upside down on the ceiling, and the floor felt mushy, almost like it had turned into a swamp from years of not being cleaned.

They found a library of sorts, though it looked like Matt the Wizard used the room mostly for costumes. Bobert counted at least six wigs hanging on the back of chairs and on candleholders on the wall. There were bookshelves, side tables, and lamps around the room, and a couple of comfortable-looking recliners that Bobert took note of to use for barricading. Or maybe for napping, if they ended up staying at the castle a long time. There was also a little stage set up for puppet shows, with puppets that loosely resembled Matt, the parrot, and the cat. Bobert pictured the wizard putting on puppet performances for his pets, or maybe making someone put one on for him. There was something very funny about that image, but Bobert also felt a touch of sadness. Could loneliness drive people to evil schemes? If so, what did that mean for Bobert?

"We should get back to the courtyard before the parrot and the cat notice we're gone," Sylvinthia said. "Quickly. Matt could be back at any moment."

Bobert didn't hear what Sylvinthia said, though. He had

turned to examine the books on the shelves, a habit he'd picked up from his mom, who always said that the first thing you should do in someone's house to get to know them was see what kind of books they had. Bobert saw a lot of dusty cooking books meant for beginners (*The Wizard's Guide to One-Pan Meals!*), a series of books called History of Evil Schemes, which were dog-eared, and then a whole bunch of coloring books that had been filled out, if a little sloppily.

Then one book caught his eye. It didn't stand out in shape or color or size. It had an interesting title (*Totally a Real Book* by Em I. Wright), but that wasn't what Bobert had noticed. He'd noticed how much less dusty it was than the other books around it.

It was a little higher than he could reach comfortably. He went up on his tiptoes, but still could only brush the bottom of the spine. Sylvinthia rolled her eyes and stepped over to help him. "Why this one?" she started asking, but before she could finish talking or pulling the book off the shelf, they heard a loud mechanical whirring, and the bookcase split in two, opening to reveal a secret set of stairs.

"Cool!" Bobert said, unable to contain himself.

"Very," Sylvinthia agreed.

Bobert took a step toward the secret stairs, but Sylvinthia put a hand on his shoulder to stop him. "Don't. What if it's a trap?"

Bobert thought about this for a second, at first scared by the idea that he could fall into another trap and get extra cursed. Then he remembered: *Be brave.* "We're his army. He probably doesn't want to hurt us. And if it was dangerous, he would have cast a spell to make sure we didn't get in, right?"

Sylvinthia chewed on her lip. "I don't think we should go. We have to prepare the barricade."

Bobert took a breath. What she was saying made a lot of sense.

"Let's just see what's there," he suggested. "Maybe there's a way out of the tunnel. Or something else that can help us."

Sylvinthia turned back toward the hall they'd come in from. She looked uncertain, even if she was equally intrigued by the staircase. "Okay," she said finally. "Two minutes, though. Then we have to tell the others."

Part of Bobert was ashamed to feel any sort of excitement in that moment. This was a serious situation: at stake was his safety and that of his fellow trapped kids, maybe even the safety of the entire kingdom. If Matt succeeded in this evil scheme—which Bobert had to admit felt at the same time completely silly and completely plausible—who knew how much damage he would cause to the people of Nefaria? He clearly had strong magical abilities, and some really zany ideas. Combining those two things could lead to some dangerous situations.

Bobert hadn't been alive that long, but even he remembered

the time a witch had made all noodles in the kingdom come to life. It sounded like a funny, wacky thing. But then anyone eating noodles at the time—which at any given moment in Nefaria, and in any gastronomically well-versed kingdom, is a lot of people—suddenly started getting attacked by their dinners. The noodles suddenly wanted more than anything not to be eaten. So they fought back against their would-be devourers, slithering back out from their mouths, curling themselves around necks, attacking Nefarians over and over again all over the kingdom. To this day, some people still refused to eat noodles.

Bobert stepped gingerly down the steps. Sylvinthia followed behind, a hand on his shoulder. It was funny how someone else putting a hand on your shoulder could make you feel more real, more present.

About halfway through, the stairway started getting dark, making it hard to tell what was ahead. They moved to the wall, feeling their way along by using the cool stone as support.

"I wish I had one of those floating torches," Bobert said.

"Shh," Sylvinthia said. "We don't know what's down there."

Bobert hadn't even thought of that. He tried tiptoeing the rest of the way, and perking his ears. Except he was a human, not a cat; he couldn't actually perk his ears. A few steps later they were in almost complete darkness. Bobert looked behind him, and it seemed like the light of the room above was much farther away then it should have been. They hadn't been walking down the stairs that long, had they? He had to remind himself to keep being brave.

Sylvinthia noticed Bobert looking back. "Do you think we should turn around?"

"No," Bobert said, so quickly he was kind of surprised by the words. "We should find out what's in here. It could be helpful."

"How are we going to find something helpful if we can't even see anything?"

Bobert started tapping his foot out in front of him, because he couldn't find the next step. "I think we reached the bottom," he said. "Maybe there's a window or a light switch."

"What's a light switch?" Sylvinthia asked.

"Oh, it's a little thing on the wall, and when you flip it, magic turns on a torch in the room so you can see." Bobert had to remind himself that he was lucky to live in a home with certain magical and technological advancements he sometimes took for granted. Not everyone at his school, and definitely not everyone in Nefaria, was that lucky. Especially not kids from the past, like Sylvinthia was.

He kept feeling at the wall, searching for the little switch. A wizard was very likely to have one, since he could set it up himself and not have to pay for it. He didn't know how else Matt would be able to see in this room.

"He probably just brings in the floating torch with him," Sylvinthia said, as if reading his mind.

But then Bobert felt the wall turn into a corner, and his fingers found a familiar piece of wood sticking out of the wall. He turned and smiled at Sylvinthia, but he hadn't flipped the switch yet, so it was dark and she couldn't see. He shook his head at himself, which thankfully she couldn't see either, and then flipped on the light.

MORE BOOKS?" Sylvinthia exclaimed. "Why would some-one build a secret room and hide it behind a library bookcase, only to hide more books?"

She was right. This was weird. The room looked almost identical to the one they had just left. One exception stood out to Bobert right away. Instead of the stage set up for puppet shows, there was a huge book resting on a stand. Also, the recliners were polka-dotted. *That* was a really bold choice. Even Bobert—whose taste apparently wasn't much better than Matt's—could tell. It made sense that Matt would hide *those* down there in the dark.

"Hey, look over here," Sylvinthia said. She was examining the shelves to the left, apparently not noticing the big book, which was the only thing really holding Bobert's attention. Aside from those awful chairs. "I think these are all magic books."

Bobert turned to the closest case. He read the title on the spine out loud. *"101 Knock-Knock Jokes That Also Serve As Curses."*

"Love, Potions, and You," Sylvinthia read out.

They made eye contact and widened their eyes. The thought of Matt the Evil Wizard with his tangled hair and dirty robes trying to use love potions on people was both funny and a little sad. And Bobert was sharing that thought with someone else. He smiled to himself.

They kept moving around different sides of the room, reading titles out loud to each other as they approached the middle, where the big book lay open. For some reason, the titles felt funnier and funnier to him. They didn't feel like powerful and scary recipes for magical disaster, or like weapons of wizardly destruction. Maybe it was because Bobert kept picturing Matt reading them, trying to make them work, and there was just something inherently silly about the man. Even if he had managed to trap Bobert and the others.

Sylvinthia caught her breath from a giggle fit after reading out a few of the chapter titles from a book called *Using Flowers for Attack Spells.* "Maybe this is why it took him so long to get his scheme to work. I don't think a wizard who's good at magic would need all these."

At some point it had started feeling safe in that weird little basement library. Like everything was in the past and they could already look back and laugh at it. Bobert still had his eye on the big book, though, and he started making his way toward it. "How long were you in the gumball machine?" Bobert asked.

Sylvinthia sighed and closed the flower book, putting it back where she'd found it on the shelf, then squatting to look at more titles below. "It's hard to tell. I don't know what year it is," she said. Her husky voice echoed in the big room.

Bobert stopped. He was in front of the big book already, but hadn't looked down at the page that was in front of him. "Oh. I hadn't even thought of that." He looked at her, waiting to read the expression on her face. He didn't know how she felt about not knowing the year, and he wanted to know before saying anything else.

She kept scanning the shelves, though, her back mostly turned away from him.

"Do you want to know?"

Bobert waited for a long time for her to answer. Finally she just shook her head. "I just want to know why."

"Why what?"

"Why no one came to look for us. Where were my parents? Where was the kingdom for the last however many years?"

They fell quiet again, especially because Bobert didn't know what to say. He turned down to look at what was on the pages in front of him. His brain didn't immediately make sense of the words. He was still thinking of what Sylvinthia had said, and wondering how long she'd been stuck in a gumball machine.

Then his brain started processing what his eyes were seeing: Spells to trap children and train armies. Spells to control others. Spells to make someone harm someone else. He realized that this was what they'd been looking for: some clue that might help them break the curse.

But before he could scan the entire page, some noises from upstairs echoed down the staircase. He and Sylvinthia both looked at each other, eyes wide. They went completely still, hoping that whatever it was would pass.

Then they heard it again, and to Bobert, at least, it seemed clear: it was squawking, and it was getting closer.

"What do we do?" Bobert whispered. He was crouching behind the bookstand now.

Sylvinthia, too, had pressed herself up against the bookshelves around the corner from the stairs. "Flip the switch again!"

"Children!" A squawk echoed down the stairwell. "I highly advise you not to be doing childish things like sneaking around and snooping! I'll be forced to call Matt." It sounded like Camila the parrot wasn't yet in the secret library, but she was almost there. If she saw the lights, they'd be goners.

But Bobert wanted to keep reading the book. If there were spells there to control the kids, and if that was how Matt was going to turn them into the army, then maybe there was information there to help the kids fight against the spells.

"Children!" Camila squawked again.

She was getting closer, and Sylvinthia was right: they had to turn the lights off. Bobert tried to look at the page one more time, to see if he could get any good tips to share with the others, but Sylvinthia shook her head. "We have to get back upstairs!"

Bobert nodded. He imagined Matt searching through some of the books around this room trying to find the most terrible punishment that existed. But this whole time Bobert also kept thinking *Be brave, be brave.* So he looked down at the page number the book was open to, then sprinted as quickly as he could to the switch by the stairs, repeating the number over and over again so he wouldn't forget it.

As soon as he flipped it, they were shrouded in darkness again. Bobert could hear his heart pounding in his ears, and he tried not to breathe too hard. He kept his eyes on the stairwell. It looked like a much longer climb back up than it had felt going down.

Suddenly, the bird appeared in the little square of light, flapping its wings to stay afloat. It cawed loudly. "Children?"

Bobert held his breath, trying not to move the slightest bit. He knew birds had good vision, but did they also have night vision? And did parrots count in that good-vision category, or just birds of prey, like eagles and hawks? Bobert turned to where he knew Sylvinthia was, but he couldn't see or hear her, which he felt was a good sign. Maybe they would get away with this.

Then the bird squawked, "Why is this bookcase open?"

Bobert closed his eyes. Oh no. The lights didn't even matter, because the stairwell itself was supposed to be hidden behind a bookcase. The bird was going to know something was up, and she would tell Matt. She would probably wait there until Bobert and Sylvinthia climbed out, and Matt would punish them. Bobert didn't want to picture what kind of punishments Matt would think up, but his brain couldn't help it: He'd throw them into a pit of snakes. He'd have a bunch of floating feathers tickle them to death. He'd make them into flying goatpoop target practice.

For the first time since the whole ordeal started, Bobert felt angry at himself. Angry for being so hungry to fit in that he'd put himself in this situation. That he'd accepted Stanbert's dare on Jennizabeth's behalf, as if that would make any of them like him. That he'd acted without thinking about what would happen if the curse was real. Now here he was, trapped in an evil wizard's secret basement library and about to be poop target practice. He should have just gone home, should have just been happy to have his parents, to have the pretty walk to and from school, to have his dad's goat stew. He should have just stayed safe and lonely.

Then Camila the parrot squawked loudly and muttered to herself, "Stupid forgetful wizard. How hard is it to close a door? To slide a bookcase back to its original position?"

And with that, she flapped her wings and left the room.

14

BY THE TIME CANDELABRA made it back home from the restaurant, it was evening.

She went to the kitchen first to grab herself a glass of water, and then to the living room, where she plopped into her favorite chair in front of the fireplace. Her eyes went to the painting above the mantel. It was a landscape scene of a pretty prairie, a cottage, and some woods with an always-blue sky overhead and a creek in the distance. Candelabra often wondered what it was like there. No matter how many times Sandraliere described it to her, Candelabra couldn't put herself in her sister's shoes. Not that she totally wanted to.

Now Candelabra saw Sandraliere approaching from the creek. It would take her a few minutes to get close enough to talk.

So Candelabra was free to think about how she wasn't going to give up. She was going to find out where that evil wizard lived, and what he was doing hanging out with someone as great as Imogene Petunias. She was going to get to the bottom of whatever his scheme was. And she was sure that was what this was, could feel it deep down in her bones.

"Hey, sis," Sandraliere said. She was drying her hair with a towel. "Any luck today?"

"No," Candelabra grumbled.

"Okay, well, take it easy. Get some rest. Did you do your homework?"

"My homework is to rescue Bobert from the evil scheme."

Sandraliere sighed. They'd had this conversation plenty of times already.

"Did you have dinner?"

"Mm-hmm, had a late lunch" Candelabra responded. She usually tried to make the most of these evenings with Sandraliere. She couldn't move the painting, otherwise she'd bring her sister with her everywhere. But tonight she was thinking of where Bobert might be stuck.

Candelabra decided to do some homework. Not actual work she needed to do for school, although she had plenty of that. She was going to do some research on this Matt guy. She opened up her wizard tablet, angling it away so that Sandraliere couldn't see the screen.

The tablet was a gift she'd gotten for her birthday from the We're Sorry You Were Involved in an Evil Scheme Committee.

Candelabra mostly used it for games, or to talk with Jennizabeth, since she also had one and they could video-chat that way. But she didn't feel like talking to anyone right now.

She opened up the Nefarianet and typed "Matt evil wizard" into the search bar.

The first thing she saw was a list of the worst names for an evil wizard. It was a theoretical list, so they weren't even talking about him specifically; someone had just guessed.

Then she saw a couple of news articles from the *Nefarious Times*. The first was from just a few years ago, and it was an opinion piece about how the people of Nefaria had to remain vigilant for evil schemes. *We've had a good run in the last few years of not having to deal with anything particularly evil*, the article read,

> *or at least no evil schemes that were particu-*
>
> *larly successful. There are always the low-level*
>
> *attempts—we all remember the sad venture by*
>
> *one so-called evil wizard named Matt to trick*
>
> *everyone in Nefaria to sign a piece of paper*
>
> *declaring him the new king—but those are*

dangerous in their own right: they make us

think evil schemes can all be laughed off.

The worry I have is that we have lived

through so many failed attempts in Nefaria

that we might not recognize a scheme that has

a legitimate chance of completely altering our

lives forever, for the worse.

Candelabra had a sinking feeling in her stomach, though she didn't fully understand it. Was it about Bobert? Or was it about the fact that adults seemed to have such a bad grasp on running things? How were evil schemes still a thing? If she were in charge, she'd do away with all that. Just let good people be the ones in charge of making decisions.

Of course, she knew it wasn't that easy.

She thought of herself as a good person, and yet she had made a bad decision a year ago. A decision that had felt innocent at the time. Not just innocent, but like a nice thing to do for her sister, who loved art and spent a lot of energy taking care of her.

It had happened after school one day, while she was waiting for Sandraliere to get off work at the school where she was an art teacher and coach of the water-balloon fight team. That school was closer to town, and Candelabra liked exploring the stores as she waited.

That day there had been a little pop-up market, and what kid who liked shopping could be blamed for thinking, *Ooh, fun!* instead of *Danger!*

She'd seen some pretty bracelets, and a hot-sauce stand where she had been allowed to try them all. Then she spotted a stand that—when she looked back on it now—was not as well lit as the others, and had a bit of an evil smell. But maybe that was just in her memory.

Anyway, there was a guy in a three-piece suit in front of some blank canvases. Candelabra didn't know how many pieces suits were supposed to have, but now she didn't trust any guy in any suit, no matter how many pieces.

He said that he was selling an exciting opportunity for artists. The canvases he was selling were enchanted, and they'd make sure that whoever painted on them would tap into their talent. It wasn't the kind of magic that would feel like cheating; it would only tap into the talent that was already there. And it was for a very good price, too.

Candelabra had reached into her bag, thrilled to do something nice for her sister, who had been her guardian for five years now.

She carried the canvas home, practically skipping. She'd gotten a little nervous that Sandraliere wouldn't want an enchanted gift, but when Candelabra gave it to her, Sandraliere burst into happy tears and pulled her sister in for the longest hug they'd had in years.

For the next few weekends, Candelabra would accompany Sandraliere to the meadow while she painted her landscape. Sometimes she would bring a book with her, or just enough snacks to not get bored. Other times she would look at her sister and think to herself that she was lucky.

Then came the day when Sandraliere was going to finish. They were at home; Sandraliere was just adding the last few strokes of color. She told Candelabra to come near and watch her apply the last swath of blue to the sky.

As soon as Sandraliere finished painting her landscape, she was sucked inside, and the painting affixed itself to the closest wall. Which at least was over the fireplace, where it tied the room together nicely.

Of course, Candelabra hadn't know that the enchantment on the canvas wasn't what the guy had said at all. He was an amateur artist himself, jealous of anyone else who painted, whether they were successful or not. In an attempt to lessen his imagined competition, he'd had the paintings enchanted to trap other artists.

Even though she hadn't known, it was the worst decision of Candelabra's life, one that haunted her even after the evildoer from that day had been sent to a rehabilitation center meant to make people less evil.

Who knew, maybe she'd made another bad decision a few days ago when the gumball machine disappeared. It could have disappeared *because* she'd made a bad decision.

The second article she read now was much older. So old that Candelabra scrolled back up to the date three different times to make sure she hadn't read it wrong. It was over a hundred years old. The headline read **LOCAL WIZARD ARRESTED ON CONSPIRACY CHARGES**. Below the headline was a picture in black-and-white of Matt in handcuffs. He was clearly the same wizard she and Bobert's parents had seen earlier that day. He looked a little younger, she guessed, but not much better. Two knights were holding him, one on either side, and the picture had captured him screaming in the direction of someone just beyond the camera. His robes were dirty, just like today.

Candelabra had always known that wizards lived a long time, that they were ancient beings. But it was a little unnerving to see the proof of it: to have seen him in the flesh a few hours ago, and now to see evidence of him existing a long time ago.

She kept reading the article. It was all about how the king's detectives had been following this wizard for a long time because he'd been purchasing suspicious materials in bulk (whole bags of witches' hair, pounds of peanut butter, bucketfuls of nail clippings of giants). They suspected him of putting together some sort of evil stew or potion. When they finally had enough evidence to storm his castle, they caught him red-handed.

"This isn't the last you've heard of Matt the Evil Wizard!" the article quoted him as saying, before he was dragged off to jail for ten years (a relatively short amount of time in the life span of a wizard). "I have many more schemes up my sleeve. I have so many schemes, they're not just in my sleeves—they're all over my robes! I have schemes up and down my pants! I will make you love me!"

Candelabra bit her lip. She kept searching the Nefarianet all night, long after the sun went down and her sister had gone to bed in the little cottage in her painting (though it always remained sunny on that side of the picture frame). Candelabra had promised that she was just finishing an assignment and she'd go to sleep soon. But that didn't happen for a long time.

It seemed that since Matt's trial and jailing, he'd been lying low and keeping out of trouble. Although Candelabra had a sneaking suspicion that he wouldn't be staying out of trouble long.

The biggest piece of information she learned that night was quite simple. But it filled Candelabra with hope, because it gave her something to do. Some way to keep searching for Bobert. She'd found—labeled simply and for the whole world to discover—Matt's castle. It was right there on Nefaria Maps, listed as a business. It had an average rating of two stars. One guy from the Kingdom of Jovialla had given it one star and written, "This guy's a jerk."

Candelabra was pretty sure the reviewer was right. And tomorrow she might find out exactly how much of a jerk Matt was.

BOBERT AND SYLVINTHIA managed to sneak back up to the library and shut the bookcase without anyone seeing. Bobert took a moment to close his eyes and sit in the relief that they'd escaped. He wasn't going to become poop target practice, wasn't going to become a wizard's new torture victim. At least not yet. "Are you coming?" Sylvinthia asked.

Bobert opened his eyes and nodded. He was still visible, too. He and Sylvinthia even kept joking around as they took a quick lap of the rest of the castle (the parts not blocked off by a spell) before rejoining the other kids in the courtyard. Jarrediah and Javitopher hadn't discovered much of interest. They'd grabbed some branches for barricading, but then the cat had started watching them with those judgmental squinty cat eyes, so they had put them down on the ground to pick up later.

"What did you guys find?" Jarrediah asked them.

"I think we have enough furniture to block all the doors,"

Sylvinthia said. "There aren't that many entrances to the castle, so if we all storm it at the same time, we could probably get it done too quickly for the bird to send a warning. I think we should start telling everyone right now."

"We also found a secret room!" Bobert said. "There were a bunch of magic books there, and I think one book that . . ."

The other kids weren't paying attention to him, though. They were talking about how to spread the word, and if they had enough food inside to barricade for long. He bit his lip and listened.

"That's something we'll have to figure out later," Sylvinthia said. "For now, the important thing is to not let the jerk back in."

Javitopher raised his hand, like he was in school. "This might sound like a silly question, but why not? Why don't we just let him do his whole plan, and then we'll be in charge *with* him?"

"You really want to be on that guy's side?" Jarrediah shot back.

"Well, I don't know if I'm on Nefaria's side," Javitopher answered. "They just left me here. So what do I care who's in charge?"

"Don't you think that has something to do with the spell?" Sylvinthia answered. "He's a doofus, but he's clearly powerful. Maybe they looked for us and the castle is invisible. Maybe it's really well hidden. Nefaria didn't trap us in the gumball machine—he did."

"But we're not *in* the gumball machine anymore," Javitopher said. "We're here. And it's all that kid's fault!" Then he pointed at Bobert, who felt his cheeks flush as the kids' voices grew with chatter.

Fortunately, Sylvinthia quieted everyone down by speaking over them. "This is better than the gumball machine. And better than *this* would be actual freedom. So let's stop arguing and try to find a way to get free."

Thankful, Bobert wanted to bring up the book again, and how it might hold the key to breaking the spell. But the other kids started arguing with one another about whether or not they would have to kill other people, and no one heard him. Maybe that didn't matter. He could just go get the book himself.

Around the courtyard, a lot of kids were sleeping, even though it was the middle of the afternoon. Bobert assumed it was out of boredom. He wondered what they'd done all those years inside the gumball machine. Could they eat? Go to the bathroom? Time obviously didn't tick forward normally in there, since they were all still kids, so how did everything else work?

He turned to Sylvinthia to ask her about that, but she started talking first. "Okay, we'll split up again, each taking a corner of the courtyard. At sundown we rush the castle.

Bobert, everyone you tell is going to block the front door, so tell them to really rush. I'll take the back entrance. Jarrediah and Javitopher, you're going to take the windows. You can use the branches to try to board them up."

"Uh," Jarrediah said, scratching his head. "We don't have a hammer or nails. And—"

"Again, we'll figure that part out later. For now the most important part is organizing the others. Everyone ready?"

Bobert thought about interrupting her and bringing up the book of spells, but he figured that once they were inside, he'd get a better chance to look at the book again. "Ready," he said, excited that they were using his idea.

"Ready," the others confirmed.

They split up and Bobert went around to his corner of the courtyard. He took a deep breath, nervous but happy, despite it all, to not be invisible. He missed his parents, missed his home; he even missed that lonely walk to and from school. But he did not miss the loneliness of being around people who didn't see him. He wasn't sure if the kids here were friends; he didn't get the sense of hope he'd gotten with Candelabra, Stanbert, and Jennizabeth right before it all went wrong. But at least he wasn't nonexistent.

He started spreading word of the plan. The kids who were on their own were easy enough to talk to. They seemed a little grumpy, but most of them agreed to it pretty quickly, maybe just because it gave them something to do. Or maybe it was an innate Nefarian urge to fight evil schemes.

There were a few little groups that were harder to convince. They seemed just happy to be out of the gumball machine. They could run; they could feel the fresh air on their faces and in their hair.

"Maybe it's better to just do what that dude says," the aggressive eight-year-old Bobert had seen in line that first day said. "I don't want him to stick us back in that thing."

He sighed and waited, and eventually almost everyone was on board with the plan. The few who didn't want to fight back changed their minds because they didn't want to be left outside the castle if everyone else was going to be inside.

The only thing left to do was wait until sundown.

Elsewhere in the kingdom, Matt woke up in one of his best moods ever.

It was a little too early, and he had to pee, which was annoying because he was very comfortable. But even with that, Matt felt elated, and ready to jump out of bed. The feeling had been building up ever since Imogene said yes to him. The thought that his army would be trained by her, that he finally had his army, that his plan was all coming together—it was almost too much to contain. He would soon take over Nefaria. His lifelong dream was going to come true. He wouldn't have to be alone in his castle anymore, with two pets he loved but who mostly seemed to tolerate him.

He practically danced out the door of his inn room. It had been a three-day walk to get to Imogene, and they were on their last day back. Matt hadn't walked that long since . . . well, maybe ever. He wasn't a big fan of walking.

In a few hours, though, probably by sundown, he'd be back at his castle, and the training would begin.

Imogene was out in the field in front of the inn, doing her morning calisthenics. Matt waved to her, but she pretended not to see him. He didn't care. Nothing could ruin his mood. He was finally going to rule Nefaria.

CANDELABRA TRIED TO CONVINCE HER SISTER that she did not have to go to school that day, that she wanted to continue the search for Bobert (though she didn't tell her exactly what her plan was, fearing that Sandraliere would try to keep her from going to Matt's castle). Sandraliere insisted that she go back, so Candelabra sat through a whole day of classes, unable to pay attention to a single thing going on.

What made it worse was that no one else cared. In her Nefarian History class, the teacher said Bobert's name when taking attendance, but then frowned at her sheet of paper and said, "That's weird. Is there a new student named Bobert here?" No one answered, not even Candelabra, who didn't want to get into it all over again.

Instead she looked at her wizard tablet under her desk, mapping the route to Matt's castle, trying to figure out what the best approach would be. Should she pretend to be selling chocolates? But then she might only be able to see a little bit inside the castle, which was unlikely to be where he was keeping Bobert, if he had him. . . .

Part of her knew that that was a big if. But that was the part of her that hadn't suspected the scam artist last time; it was the part of her that was prone to fall for evil schemes if she let her guard down; and she decided it was the part of her that she wanted to listen to the least. She wanted to listen to the parts of her that were cautious about evil schemes, and would never fall for one again.

"Candelabra, are you listening?"

She almost dropped her tablet. The whole class was looking at her now, especially Mr. Gobbledegook and his out-of-control eyebrows.

"Mm-hmm," she said, even though already her mind was thinking about sneaking into the castle from the back. She'd zoomed in on Nefaria Maps as close as she could, and she could tell there was a wall surrounding the entire compound. But usually those stone walls had plenty of nooks and crannies to get fingers and feet into, so climbing it wouldn't be that difficult.

"I'm sure you are. Wizard tablet away, please," he said.

At lunch, she sat next to Jennizabeth and Stanbert as usual, but they didn't share one another's meals like always, and didn't talk about how much of a jerk Professor Blort was. Jennizabeth was almost as chatty as usual, but when she talked about her weekend, it was clear that she was doing it to cover up the weirdness of what had happened, and the fact that Candelabra hadn't been there. They almost always hung out on the weekends. But of course Candelabra had been searching for Bobert.

"Wanna go to town after school?" Jennizabeth asked.

Candelabra was back to examining Matt's castle on her tablet, trying to get a sense for how many rooms it had, and how she could get into them to search for Bobert in every little corner of it.

"What are you looking at?" Stanbert asked, trying to look over at the tablet.

Candelabra shut it quickly and put it away in her backpack, turning her attention to the boiled meat in a bag that was her lunch. "No, I can't today," Candelabra said. "Homework."

They fell quiet again, all of them knowing that they were in the same classes, and that they barely had any homework to do.

Finally the end-of-day bell rang, and Candelabra was free to go. She had told Sandraliere that after school she was going to play frees-bees (a game where kids freed a box of angry bees and ran away, and the person who got stung the least won), so that left her plenty of time to go to Matt's castle before raising suspicions. She had, just in case, though, left a note tucked under her pillow saying who she was and where she was going to go. She figured that if Matt, silly-seeming though he was, had somehow managed to trap Bobert and erase him from everyone's memories, he could do the same to her.

She gathered her belongings and practically ran out the door, heading toward the path in the woods that led to town. She did stop at the candy shop for a moment to get a handful of chocolate bars. She hadn't eaten much at lunch, and she needed the energy. Plus, the spider monkeys who ran it were always so friendly, and she wanted to make sure someone saw her going toward town. Again, she wanted to be careful, to leave a trace of where she'd gone.

In almost record time, she got to the end of the path. At the break in the trees, where the town became visible, she took a moment to catch her breath and drink some water. She looked at the familiar scene: the landscape, the market, the town square, the king's castle. And all the other castles peppered around the land, belonging to various lords and duchesses and that one strange family of clowns that was simply rich enough to buy a castle.

Of course, she was only looking for one specific castle. One that she might have not paid any mind before. She pulled out her tablet to double-check where it was, then looked back up at the land. Yes, almost directly across from her. She'd have to go down into the valley, cross town, then head back up the mountain.

The castle was in a flat stretch along the slope, though it

was hard to tell that, because it was surrounded by trees. She could see the exterior wall she'd have to climb (she'd decided sneaking in was the best approach, and if she got caught, she could use some of the chocolate bars as an excuse and pivot to the whole salesperson thing). There was a single turret that rose above the treetops. It probably had a nice view of town, but even from where she was, Candelabra could tell it wasn't in the best shape. There were no pretty vines wrapped around it, not even the kind without leaves.

"There you are!"

Candelabra whipped around, taken by surprise at Stanbert's voice. He was with Jennizabeth, and they were sweaty as they approached her.

"What are you doing here?" she asked them, ignoring the fact that this was the path to Jennizabeth's house.

"We followed you," Jennizabeth panted. "Why were you going so fast?"

"Why did you follow me? You shouldn't have done that!"

Stanbert pulled out his water pouch and took three big gulps. "You're still trying to find him, aren't you?"

Candelabra crossed her arms and turned away from them. She started stomping her way down the hill, hoping they were too tired to chase her, too tired to try to talk her out of her plan.

"Candy, wait!" Stanbert said. "We want to help!"

She stopped again. For some reason it almost made her

want to cry, the fact that they had chased her all this way not to stop her but to help. "Why?"

"We believe you," Jennizabeth said. "If you say he's missing, that there's something evil going on, then we can't let you look for him on your own."

Candelabra's best friend smiled at her, and they walked toward each other and hugged.

"So, what's the plan?" Stanbert said. "But don't answer until we've rested. You are too fast."

17

BY THE TIME THEY MADE IT all the way across the valley, it was close to sundown. Candelabra thought back to the day they'd spent at the town square, waiting for twilight to test out the curse. She tried to insert Bobert into the memory, convinced at this point that he had been there with them. Maybe he had always been with them.

She shook away the memories, or lack thereof, telling herself there was no point in thinking about that. She was fixing what had gone wrong. She was going to rescue Bobert.

Once they were getting close to the castle, they left the road and dipped into the woods so no one would see them coming. They had to go all the way around to the back of the castle anyway. Even more leaves had fallen in the days since Bobert had disappeared, and it was hard not to think that each crunch of the leaves beneath their boots might give them away.

"Shh!" Candelabra called out to her friends, even though she was crunching just as many leaves as they were.

After too long trying and failing to move in perfect silence, they could see the stone wall at the edge of the compound. The turret was high above them, and Candelabra motioned for them all to crouch and stay in the cover of the trees.

"Are you sure you want me to stay out here?" Jennizabeth asked. "I can go in with you."

Candelabra shook her head. "If something goes wrong and we don't come out, we need someone to go tell the adults."

"This is much higher than it looked from across the valley," Stanbert said, staring up at the stone wall.

"Yeah," Candelabra agreed. Then she wove her fingers together and formed her hands into a flat surface for Stanbert to step on. "You go first. You'll need the help."

Stanbert looked like he was going to disagree. But even though he wasn't as small as other kids in the class (if she'd been able to remember him, Candelabra would have thought of Bobert, who was the shortest kid in their grade), she was definitely taller and stronger than him. He shrugged and put a boot into her hands. Candelabra lifted him up, and he reached as high as he could. A part of her was afraid that he wouldn't be able to reach the top, but another part of her was afraid that he would. That they were actually going to have to pull off a rescue mission for a kid who maybe didn't exist.

Then his fingers gripped the edge, and he was able to pull himself up.

ADI ALSAID

"Well?" Candelabra called up.

At first he seemed to be too worried about getting himself onto the top of the wall to look inside the courtyard. But once he was up there, flat on his belly, gripping either side of the wall with his hands, he turned and got his first glance inside.

It wasn't quite what he was expecting. He thought it'd be a bit of a run-down yard. Maybe there'd be a rusty basketball hoop that hadn't been used in a long time. A lot of tall grass and maybe a scummy fountain. At worst he thought this supposed Bobert kid might be there, tied to a post or something. Maybe there'd be a dog, because even evil wizards had pets, right?

Instead, what he saw was kids. A lot of them. Hundreds, probably. And they were all, in that exact moment, running away from him and toward the castle.

Even though he was pretty much one of the leaders of the whole plan, Bobert let all the other kids run ahead of him. He wasn't a very fast runner, and he always had a slight fear of being trampled, because he was so small. Plus, the other kids were louder when they yelled, "Now!" So he let them all sprint toward the castle while he jogged behind, unaware of Stanbert and Candelabra scaling the wall behind him.

The kids were all letting loose a war cry, really storming the castle, even though it was empty. That hadn't been part of the plan. But Bobert understood why it felt like the right move. Especially given how long those kids had been stuck inside the gumball machine. They hadn't had the chance to run in so long, hadn't had the chance to scream and let their voices be heard by others. They were being brave, Bobert thought admiringly. Imogene Petunias would applaud for them, if she could see them.

He was one of the last to make it into the castle. The yells were even louder inside, bouncing off the walls. He felt momentarily bad for the cat, who was probably terrified.

He made eye contact with Sylvinthia, who was waiting for everyone to make it through the door. The others had already gathered a couple of chairs from nearby rooms, as well as the three finger-gun portraits from the great hall. She nodded at him, then slammed the door shut behind. "Go, go, go!" she yelled.

Bobert did what he was told and ran through the castle toward the front. It was hard to keep track of who was supposed to be going there with him. He hadn't had the chance to learn all the kids' names yet, or remember their faces. Plus, it was complete mayhem inside the castle. Some kids were running very purposefully toward furniture and helping one another move it to a specific location. Other kids were trying to move furniture without knowing where they were taking it. Some kids were just running around waving their hands in the air and screaming. Still others kept trying to break into areas protected by Matt's spells, and they kept bouncing off, over and over again.

Bobert didn't have time to help them calm down. He had to get to the front door and make sure it was barricaded. After that, things would be a lot less frantic. After this plan worked—*his plan*—the others would fully include him. And then they'd listen to him and go back to the secret room with the spell book, where all of this would be undone and he would return home. Candelabra and the others would know that he was brave, and he wouldn't be alone anymore.

For now, though, there was still a lot of activity. Glass was breaking everywhere. Sylvinthia's voice somehow carried through the castle: "If you break a window, make sure you cover it up! Don't give him any way to come in!"

Bobert made his way through the dining room, where ten kids were trying to push the massive table, though it was hard to tell where they wanted it to go. They might not have talked about it at all, because in the brief time Bobert was passing through the dining room, it definitely looked like they made two steps of progress in one direction before they started moving in the other. The result was that the table wasn't moving at all. "Follow me!" Bobert yelled at them.

He didn't bother looking behind to see if they were listening. He wanted to make sure the front door was closed, and at least a little barricaded. He could worry about fortifying it once he got there.

He passed the kitchen and was through the second hall when he heard squawking coming behind him. He looked over his shoulder as he ran, and indeed Camila the parrot was following. Her talons were extended, too, as if she wanted to swoop him up.

He ran even faster, trying to remember the exact way to the front of the castle. When he passed the library to his right, he figured out where he was, and sprinted ahead, maneuvering around a few other kids who were running pretty fast, sure. But they didn't have a crazed parrot coming after them, and everyone knows that you run faster when a talking parrot is trying to capture you.

Finally, he saw it up ahead: the main entrance to the castle. The big wooden double doors, almost identical to the ones that faced the courtyard, and which Matt had stumbled out of that first day.

Some kids were there already, thankfully. They had only managed to put some couch cushions from the sitting room nearby in front of the door. They were younger kids, who'd probably been able to squeeze through the crowd faster than the others. But they couldn't move Matt's old, heavy, and mostly tasteless furniture.

Bobert felt hope surge through him. They were going to

succeed in their barricade. His idea was going to work. He would have time to go read that book of spells and break the curse. He would get to go home. The others would get to go home. If they still had homes. Even if they didn't, they would be free, and it would be thanks to him.

He just had to glance over his shoulder one more time as he ran to make sure that annoying bird wasn't going to claw his face off or anything. When he saw that he was farther away from Camila than the last time, he felt proud of his speed, proud that he was going to succeed at this, at least. Then he faced forward again just in time to see the front door a few inches from his face.

18

THERE WAS AN ADDED JOY in Matt's heart when he saw his castle again. It wasn't just the regular joy of returning home. It was returning home having finally achieved what he'd dreamed of for so many years.

Almost, anyway. He didn't want to get too ahead of himself.

He looked over at Imogene and swept an arm toward the castle. "There it is! Isn't it a beautiful sight?"

Imogene made a noise that Matt took as a scoff of agreement, even though that wasn't really a thing people did, especially not Imogene Petunias. Imogene scoffed often, but never in agreement.

"Just wait until you see the inside! One of the finest turrets ever designed, if I do say so myself. Granted, that's *my* room. You'll be in the basement while we train. But it's fairly nice there, too, ever since we got rid of the spider's nests. Justin—that's my cat—has mostly scared the remaining rats away too! So it's in tip-top shape."

"Sounds wonderful," Imogene said. She sighed, thinking again and again, as she'd had to throughout this three-day walk, of the pie recipe. Just two more weeks of surviving this jerk and whatever cockamamie army (cockam-army?) he'd assembled, and then she would have the recipe. And her retirement would be all the sweeter for it.

They walked across the sad drawbridge that rested over the moat Matt had clearly dug himself with a shovel. To call it a moat was a little too generous. It was more of a long, skinny pond. Three sad koi fish swam in the murky brown and looked up at Imogene with eyes that seemed to beg her to take them away from that place.

At the door, Matt stopped and started patting himself all over. Imogene sighed and put her bag down. "Sorry, too many pockets in these robes," Matt muttered. "Aha, there we go!" He smiled and reached somewhere near his armpit. Then he looked at what he'd pulled out and frowned. "Frog bones. Don't remember putting those there."

He tossed them onto the ground.

That was when Imogene heard the commotion. It sounded like pounding footsteps and yelling, like an army going to war. Oh god, what had she signed up for? What was waiting for her inside that castle? She closed her eyes and remembered eating Grandma Gertrude's apple pie, trying to hold the flavor in her mouth and keep it there.

Matt was still searching for his keys when he, too, heard the noises coming from inside. He stepped closer to the door and stopped moving, trying to make sure his ears hadn't played a trick on him. But no, there was definitely some sort of mayhem happening on the other side. He tried the doorknob, just in case he'd forgotten to lock up. But it didn't budge. So he kept searching through his robes, this time with a little more urgency.

That darn Camila, Matt thought. She was a good sidekick, but he shouldn't have expected her to keep control of the children for days on end. What was going on in there? He put his ear directly on the door, trying to figure it out.

Candelabra and Stanbert sat on top of the wall for just a second, watching the mass of kids rush from the courtyard. In a matter of seconds, it had completely emptied out, leaving only a handful of kids who'd fallen asleep waiting for sundown and whom no one had thought to wake up.

"Where did they all go?" Stanbert asked.

"Forget where they went," Candelabra said. "Who were they? How are there this many kids here who no one knows about?"

As soon as she said the words out loud, Candelabra pieced it together. She turned to look at Stanbert, who was brushing himself off from his not totally perfect landing in the grass.

"What?" he asked.

"The gumball machine! The curse!"

He still didn't get it. So she did what most people do when faced with someone who doesn't get it. She put her hands on his shoulders, got closer to his face, and said it again, but louder. "The gumball-machine curse, Stanbert! It's real. It traps kids inside, and that's them. It must be!"

Stanbert looked over at the entrance to the castle, from which he could hear shouts and glass breaking and all sorts of other loud noises he couldn't even identify. A bird squawking? A cat hissing? "If that's them, why would they run away from us? And where's that Bobert kid?"

Candelabra didn't want to waste more time. She started moving toward the castle. "I don't know. But he has to be here, and we're gonna find him."

On the other side of the wall, Jennizabeth pulled out her sketchbook and some colored pencils, figuring she might as well spend her time waiting productively. She looked up at the wall, somewhat happy that she hadn't had to climb it, but a little nervous that the sun had gone down and she was going to be out there all alone in the dark soon.

No, she couldn't think about it like that. Candelabra and Stanbert would find nothing, and they'd be back in five minutes. Fifteen, tops. She sighed and took a seat, setting her sketchbook on her lap and tapping a pencil against her knee.

At the front of the castle: true mayhem.

Bobert was lying on top of the door, not entirely sure what had happened, but knowing that there was chaos around him. He could see feet all around him. He covered his head with his hands, hoping no one would crush him to death. *Be brave,* he kept thinking, *be brave.* Even though being brave had led him to knock the door off the hinges directly onto Matt, causing a stampede and messing up the plan entirely.

Matt was shouting both in pain and for someone to get the door off him.

Many of the kids, who in their quest to barricade the door had forgotten that leaving sounded like a much better option, now tried to run out the broken entrance. They'd also forgotten, however, that Matt, as silly as he was, had put protective spells around the castle. The result was a bunch of excited kids clamoring and pressing for the exit, followed by Bobert yelling as he was nearly trampled, followed by the kids bouncing off the protective spell. The bounce was accompanied by a loud *boing!* every time, which was a touch Matt had added to the spell just for fun.

☀ ⁝ ☀

Imogene stood by, observing it all, and wondering if Grandma Gertrude's apple pie was really worth all this. Whatever *this* was.

Meanwhile, inside the castle, many of the kids hadn't even noticed the door breaking and Matt arriving, and they were still trying to barricade the windows and other exits. More than a few of them, who'd spent all that time inside the gumball machine eating nothing, surviving on whatever spell Matt was using on them and the occasional mouthful of bubble gum, were tearing the kitchen to shreds. The pantry was still off-limits, and there were plenty of *boing!*s to prove it. But the icebox door was wide open, and there were four kids with their whole heads inside it, licking up any remnants of food or foodlike substances that Matt may have spilled.

In the courtyard, Candelabra and Stanbert made their way cautiously inside right as Sylvinthia yelled for the doors to shut. She was really thriving in her role as someone who yelled instructions, and hers was quickly the best-barricaded entrance to the castle. It unfortunately didn't matter, but no one told her, so she was able to feel pride for a little longer. She saw Candelabra and Stanbert walk in, and did a double take, wondering why they didn't look familiar. But then she had to turn her attention toward two boys who were trying to stack an armchair on top of a sofa.

"What is happening here?" Stanbert asked. He stayed close to Candelabra, not wanting to get swept up in the frenzy of all these kids who seemed intent on destroying everything in their sight.

"I don't know," Candelabra said. She was trying to take a good look at each kid's face, wanting to find Bobert's features there. But they were all moving too manically, or crying, and the lighting inside the castle wasn't very good. It was especially hard since she could only remember Bobert's face from a class portrait.

She called out his name a few times, but no one turned to look at her. Instead, things started to fly all around them. Not magically, but because they were being thrown. The yelling, the scrambling, the hectic rush to barricade themselves from Matt—not knowing he'd already arrived—had only built up in the cursed gumball-machine kids. They felt like they were running out of time, and in their desperation they began throwing anything near them in the general direction of the doors and the windows, hoping it would keep them safe from Matt, hoping it would be the difference in helping them break free of him once and for all.

"This doesn't feel right," Stanbert said.

"Come on," Candelabra replied. "Let's keep moving. He's gotta be here somewhere."

"Get off me!" Matt shouted.

Bobert had already rolled off the door, trying to get out of the way of the kids bouncing off the invisible shield. A few of the bigger kids came over and helped him to his feet. At first all he saw was the broken door on the floor, with just a bit of blue cloth sticking out from below. He looked back at the now-empty doorway and the splinters of wood stuck to the hinges, then down at the floor again.

"Miss Petunias!" the door shouted.

Now the crowd of kids parted, and Bobert saw a broad-shouldered woman approach. He couldn't believe it was really her. He wasn't sure if he was starstruck, or if everything that had just happened was what was making him speechless.

The famous warrior leaned down and picked up the door with both hands, propping it up against the wall by the doorway. Matt looked like he'd been literally flattened. And for a second Bobert thought that maybe he really had smooshed the wizard into the ground, and maybe Imogene would be proud of him for it.

But then Imogene reached down and grabbed two fistfuls of the wizard's robes and lifted him completely off his feet. Matt stumbled, then brushed himself off. "I can stand up by myself, thank you very much."

Imogene rolled her eyes, then crossed her arms in front of her chest. "What exactly have I signed up for?"

"You know our deal. You train my army for two weeks, you get the recipe." Now he seemed to piece together the fact that his door was broken, and his army was milling about, watching him. A few were trying to make a run for it, but they were currently *boing!*ing off his spell's force field.

Bobert couldn't believe she was really here. And that she wasn't rescuing them. She seemed, instead, to be on Matt's side.

"Please don't tell me these children are your army."

"Camila!" Matt called out, checking his elbows for scrapes that he didn't actually have. "Justin! Will someone please explain what's going on here?"

On cue, Camila the parrot landed on Matt's shoulder. Bobert had never seen a bird panting before, but that was definitely what she was doing now. "The children," she squawked. "They mutinied."

Matt sighed and stepped inside the castle, taking in the chaos that was still unfolding. He looked back and made eye contact with Bobert. "How disappointing," he said.

"I'll say," the little boy Bobert had met in line said, except it sounded like he meant it about something else.

Then Matt reached into his robe and pulled out his wand. "You're lucky this isn't broken," he said, directly to Bobert again. "Then I would be really angry."

Bobert looked away, embarrassed to be put on the spot, but

also just trying to wrap his mind around his hero standing in front of him.

His thoughts were interrupted by Matt waving his wand and saying, "Poofty goofty, everything go boofty."

And everything went black.

PART II

19

BOBERT FELT THE SUN IN HIS EYES before he opened them. He shut them even tighter, though, willing himself to fall back asleep, as if that could keep away the morning. His body was sore, even after two weeks of training. His shins were scabbed from being kicked and scraped by other kids' armor. His side was bruised from when Jarrediah had hit him during a training exercise, and just to make it worse, it was the side he liked to sleep on.

Around him he could hear the other kids waking up, shifting in their sleep sacks, pulling the thin fabric tighter around them to try to fight the brisk morning. The weather had started to shift in the past few days, and even though Matt had placed a warming spell on the courtyard, it didn't work all that well. Maybe he was straining himself with too many spells. Maybe he was getting weaker, and soon the curse would break, and they would all be free.

But Bobert couldn't get his hopes up too much.

It was the last day of full training, and there was a nervous energy in the air. The kids couldn't help but feel some excitement, and definitely some relief. Most of them didn't want to help Matt go through with his plan, but at least morning exercises would be over. And maybe they'd have better food once the invasion was done and Matt was in control of Nefaria.

Bobert didn't care. He was trying to be as invisible as possible now, and he was going to keep doing that after Matt's plan, whether it succeeded or failed. Bobert might try to be invisible the rest of his life. That was probably for the best.

Ever since the attempted mutiny, he'd been getting dirty looks and shoulder bumps, and during sparring everyone lined up to try to hit him with their various weapons. Thankfully, even with the training, a lot of the kids were still too weak to really use the weapons effectively.

Still, they pushed him out of line during meals, so that he was left with the soggiest sandwiches (which were already pretty soggy to begin with). They didn't let him sit with them for meals, moved his sleeping bag to the edge of the courtyard, and called him "genius" in a tone that made it seem like the most insulting thing someone could be called.

They were angry, and Bobert figured they had a right to be. Some of them had gotten used to life in the gumball machine, never being hungry, never aging. Sure, they weren't ever really happy there. But they had learned to quiet their hope a long time ago, and if it hadn't been for Bobert's scheme to barricade themselves in, they wouldn't have had to feel it again. Having felt hope for the first time in so long, it had hurt that much more to have it stamped down and smothered. Bobert knew that more than most.

Now, every time one of them looked at him, Bobert could see that hurt, that anger, in their eyes. He didn't think he knew what it felt like to be hated, but this felt close to it. He so wished that he could go back and be invisible again. That they would just ignore him. If he ever got out of this mess, he'd happily return to his life of walking to school and back alone. He'd get pooped on by flying goats every day if he didn't have to feel this way anymore.

Maybe being brave wasn't all it was cracked up to be. After all, not only had he made it worse for the other kids, but he had gotten Candelabra and Stanbert stuck in there with him. How, he didn't exactly know. But it was obviously his fault.

When Matt had rounded them all up after the failed attempt to lock him out, Bobert had been shocked to see Candelabra and Stanbert in a corner of the courtyard. Their eyes met, but Matt had frozen them all in place. They couldn't even wave at each other. Which maybe was a good thing, because they probably would have yelled at him for doing this to them.

For the next two weeks, as Matt and Imogene held the

kids to a rigorous training schedule under a watchful eye, Bobert tried to stay away from the others, and especially from Candelabra and Stanbert.

That first night, after Matt had unfrozen them and Candelabra and Stanbert had come out of their shock, they did approach Bobert where he'd set up his sleep sack along one of the walls.

His heart quickened when they were near, afraid that just having them talk to him would result in severe consequences for all of them. Before Candelabra could even say hello, Bobert shook his head. "It's better if I'm alone!" he said, louder than he meant to. "You should stay away from me."

They looked confused, but Bobert wasn't going to let them stick around and suffer more because of him. He grabbed his sleep sack and carried it to the other side of the courtyard, ignoring their calls behind him.

He'd spent a few days running away from them this way until they seemed to give up. At least they didn't join in on the mean looks or the insults.

They went through the last day of training as usual, with Matt asking every kid individually if they were excited for the conquest. Most didn't bother to respond as they chewed soggy grass sandwiches for lunch. Imogene led them through one last marching drill, barking orders even though Bobert could tell her heart wasn't in it, if it ever had been. He liked to think that it hadn't been. That Matt was blackmailing her somehow, or had her under some spell.

When the day was over and it was time for bed, Bobert hid by his sleeping bag until the lines for the outhouses (which Matt had put a deodorizing spell on after the kids complained), the bathroom bushes (some kids refused to go into the outhouses), and the toothbrushing area of the fountain cleared out. He'd learned which path to take to stay in the shadows the longest, which had the fewest number of kids who were confrontational. Maybe their anger toward him was cooling off, because no one tried to trip him, and he heard very few comments thrown his way.

He washed his face in the fountain, thinking his parents would be proud of him at least for that. Someone cleared their throat behind him, making him jump and open his eyes. Unfortunately it was in that order, so he tripped on the edge of the fountain and fell to the ground. When he rolled over and looked up, he saw Sylvinthia reaching her hand out to help him.

"Come on," she said. "I'm not going to bite your head off or anything."

"But you *are* going to bite me?"

She rolled her eyes and waved her hand. Bobert took it gingerly, muttering a thanks. He wanted to flee, but he had just started brushing his teeth, and that seemed like a choking hazard.

"How come you keep running away from your friends?" Sylvinthia asked.

Not a great time to have a mouth full of foam. He coughed into his hand to save it from getting all over Sylvinthia. "My what?"

"The new kids. They're your friends, right?" She narrowed her eyes at him, and Bobert turned away, continuing to brush his teeth. He didn't need to be reminded that he was to blame for everything, that he had done this to kids who barely even knew him.

"Look, I don't know your whole life story or anything. But if anyone from my life showed up here, I wouldn't care what they'd done to me or what I'd done to them. I would be running to them."

When he returned to his shoddy sleep sack, which had seemed to get thinner as the nights went on, he looked over at where Candelabra and Stanbert had set up, not too far from him. Stanbert was already snoring, only the top of his head visible from the sleeping bag's opening. Candelabra was looking up at the stars, so she didn't see it when Bobert picked up his stuff, avoided the kids still trying to trip him, and came over to her.

A part of him ached for things to be like they were the day

he got himself stuck in the machine. Those few hours of friendship. But no, he was going to be alone, and that was better.

That didn't mean he couldn't be a little closer. Avoiding Candelabra's eyes, he laid his sleep sack down and slid into it. He turned on his side, facing the stone wall, away from all the other kids. It was easier to fall asleep that way. He could pretend he was just out camping with his parents, maybe. It was some of the only joy he'd found in his last few days, using his brain to conjure up family, and home. It felt like magic.

"Is this yours?"

Candelabra had whispered so quietly that Bobert at first wasn't sure he'd actually heard anything. He shifted in his sleeping bag and looked back, expecting to see her sleeping. But she was looking right back at him, and it was a thrill.

"What?"

Candelabra lifted herself up onto her elbow to get a better look at Bobert, still whispering but raising her voice just a little bit as she stretched her free hand out. "This is gonna sound weird. But I had this in my hand, and it led me here, and . . . were we friends? Are we?"

Bobert didn't know what to say to that, so instead he looked at what was in her hand.

"I don't know what happened," Candelabra said. "But I think we were with you before you got stuck."

Her pause made him realize she was waiting for him to confirm, and so he nodded his head, still examining his eraser. "You don't remember," he whispered. Then, before the heartbreak could sink too deep, he added, "But it's my fault you're in here."

"What? How is it your fault?"

"Because I got stuck in the machine. And you got pulled in after me or whatever. I made you and Stanbert get stuck here. I made everyone get stuck here."

Candelabra didn't say anything right away, and Bobert strained to see her expression through the dark. Surely, she was angry that she was stuck in here with him. Because of him.

"Look, we don't remember exactly what happened. We were in front of the machine all of a sudden and I had this eraser in my hand. I'm guessing it's part of the curse. That when you get trapped inside, the rest of the world forgets you. I'm only sorry that I didn't see it coming. I don't know how I missed it. You probably know about my sister, right?"

She waited for Bobert to respond to that, but he was at a loss for words.

"It was my fault then and it was my fault now. Stanbert and I didn't get pulled in. We came looking for you. We came to rescue you."

What does a kid do, hearing something like that? Bobert lay back down, pulling the ragged sleeping bag up to his chin, keeping his eyes on Candelabra. "Oh," he said. He smiled into the dark, unable to hide the joy that came bubbling up within him.

20

EVEN THOUGH HE DIDN'T SLEEP any longer than normal, Bobert slept the best he had since the whole getting-stuck-in-a-cursed-castle thing happened.

He felt so good, in fact, that it was a bit of a shock when he woke up to go use the bathroom bushes and the few others who were awake in the courtyard were still giving him dirty looks. They didn't cut as deep, but it was a little weird to remember that not everything had changed after talking to Candelabra. That there wasn't a misunderstanding with everyone else, too, that had also been cleared up.

Bobert went back to his sleep sack, still feeling the joy of last night's moment, just a little dampened by the realization that nothing had actually changed. And the fact that his abs were screaming with every movement, sore from yesterday's exercises.

Sure, Candelabra and Stanbert had forgotten him, like always seemed to happen. But this time it had been because of a wizard's curse, not some nameless one that the universe had assigned to Bobert. More than that, he now knew why he hadn't been rescued, why no one had come looking for all the gumball kids.

For the next hour, as the sun rose in the sky, his thoughts were racing. Bravery was on his mind again: how Candelabra and Stanbert had risked so much to try to save him, even though they didn't remember him. And maybe he had messed up when he'd tried to save the others, but that didn't mean he should give up.

Maybe what he needed was another plan to get them out. He immediately thought of the hidden room with all the spell books. He just needed a way to get there without involving anyone else. If there were risks to be taken, he would take them all alone.

"Morning," Candelabra said beside him.

"Good morning," Bobert said quietly, then cleared his throat and said it again with more confidence.

"Has he—" Candelabra started to say, but was interrupted by the worst alarm clock of all time.

Matt came out from the castle, banging a wooden spoon against a rusty old pot, which was now all dented and warped from the damage he'd done to it every morning. "Get up, soldiers! Morning calisthenics!"

Bobert groaned and sat up. Behind Candelabra, Stanbert

also sat up and stretched. "I wish he'd give us breakfast before," he said to Candelabra.

"Why? So we can throw it all up?" Candelabra grumbled.

Stanbert's hair had cowlicks in about six different places, and despite the circumstances, Bobert managed to smile at the sight. Stanbert rubbed the sleep from his eyes and let out a long, extended yawn that made him look like Justin the cat. He even curved his back in the same way and reached out a hand like it was a paw. Then he noticed Bobert and gave him a smile and a wave.

"Come on!" Matt bellowed. "Rise and shine, up and at 'em. I have a surprise for you!"

"Are you going to leave us alone?" shouted someone near the fountain in the middle of the courtyard.

Those who were already fully awake laughed. Even Bobert found himself giggling.

Matt kept banging the pot as he walked through the courtyard, a smile on his face. "Actually, that was the plan. Morning calisthenics, and then the day is yours to rest up before our campaign begins. But if anyone has any wisecracks to say to that, I'll happily rearrange the schedule."

A chorus of "Shh!" and "No, no, no!" and "Is he serious?" rang out around the courtyard. Matt was really soaking up playing the good guy, Bobert could just tell. There was again something strangely familiar about the wizard, something

Bobert couldn't put his finger on, but which made him both uncomfortable and more curious about his kidnapper.

"That's what I thought. Now get up and begin your stretching before I change my mind."

The kids now scampered to their feet, despite their sore muscles and aching bones. Bobert, as usual, took his time getting up, letting everyone else beat him to the punch. This time, though, it wasn't because he was worried about being small and getting lost in the shuffle, or anything like that. It was because, for the first time since the failed barricade, he felt a glimmer of hope. If Matt was really going to leave them alone, maybe he would have a chance to sneak into the secret library.

Now Imogene emerged from the castle, with her coffee mug in one hand and a Grandma Gertrude pie in the other, ready to lead them in the morning routine. She looked relaxed, happy that this was all coming to an end. And if even *she* was relaxed, then there was a good chance things would be quiet enough at the compound for Bobert to at least come up with a plan.

He looked over at Candelabra, who was also slowly getting out of her sleeping bag, and for the first time since he saw her in there with him, he managed a real smile.

After calisthenics and breakfast, Matt stayed true to his word and let the kids do whatever they wanted. Within the confines of the courtyard, of course. The only thing left on the schedule was a big motivational speech at dinner. Matt seemed intent on making Imogene give it, but she seemed just as intent on not giving it. "I've done my part," Bobert heard her say. "I expect my payment today, and then I'm gone."

Even though it had been disappointing to see her work for Matt, and even though they had been training against their will (whenever one of them tried to *not* train, their bodies moved anyway, improving their marching and sword-holding despite themselves), it had been kind of cool to be trained by Imogene Petunias. Not many of the other kids knew about her, since they'd been stuck in the gumball machine for so long. But Bobert, Candelabra, and Stanbert definitely knew.

Now the three of them were lying in the grass, letting their bodies recover. Stanbert was on his stomach, snoring, a tiny bit of drool dripping down onto the ground. Sylvinthia and Jarrediah were nearby too, both splayed out like starfish, letting the weak autumn sun warm their faces. They had joined them right after morning calisthenics, Sylvinthia approaching with a nod and a smile.

Bobert pulled up his pant leg to pick at the scab on his shin. He wondered if it would leave a scar, and if he would always remember his time at this stupid castle because of it. Then he realized he wouldn't need a scar to remember this. He'd been sucked into a gumball machine, then spat back out to become a pawn in an evil scheme. That's the kind of stuff you don't forget.

"How bad is Matt's speech going to be?" Candelabra asked. "Do you wanna bet how many times he calls himself 'great'?"

"A thousand," Jarrediah guessed.

"Depends on how long the speech is," Sylvinthia said. "If it's more than ten minutes, a thousand is kind of a low guess."

They all laughed, then went back to resting. Bobert looked toward the castle, thinking. Then his eyes landed on Imogene again, and he remembered every story he knew about her. The time she'd convinced the dragon to go vegetarian so it would stop eating villagers. How she'd held off the whole army from Infamia using only a sword, a shield, and three flamethrowers. How she was the greatest living warrior in Nefaria and had all the exploits to prove it. And suddenly Bobert had an idea.

APPROACHING A FAMOUS WARRIOR is probably never easy, not that Bobert had any experience doing that. Imogene Petunias was an intimidating person, not just because of her physical abilities and stature, but because of the history of everything she'd done. At that moment, though, Imogene was staring in Matt's direction, her jaw set in stone. If stones were angry.

Throughout training, she hadn't been mean to any of the kids. She was strict, and often annoyed at Matt, but Bobert guessed that the worst thing she would do now was to tell him to get lost. She still looked very angry, though, and Bobert generally didn't like approaching angry people who knew how to use weapons expertly.

He took a breath and walked over to where she was sitting on the steps leading up to the castle. If it went well, this would be one of the last walks where he had to ignore everyone who was looking at him like he was the only one to blame for the curse.

Before he knew it, he was standing in front of her. It was

one thing to be trained by her, to even have her come over and adjust his grip on his "sword" (it wasn't a sword at all, but clearly an old wooden post for something like a stop sign, just with some leather wrapped around the bottom to make a handle). But it was another thing to be directly in front of her, waiting to ask her for a favor, to convince her to help the kids. He cleared his throat, which got her attention right away.

"No more advice, kid, I'm off the clock. Remember to bend your knees."

That took the wind out of the sails of the speech he had been preparing in his mind. A part of him wanted to just hide again, go back to invisibility. But Stanbert and Candelabra had risked themselves for him, and this was the least he could do. He decided it would be best if he didn't have to look her directly in the face as he said what he wanted to say, so he took a seat next to her.

"Miss Petunias, I just wanted to ask you something."

"I'm not exactly in the mood. I just want to go home, and this jerk keeps coming up with excuses to not pay me what I'm owed."

"Hmm," Bobert said, apparently in a way that made Imogene forget about herself for a second.

"'Hmm' what?"

He hesitated, but then remembered: bravery. "I don't think you're the only one who wants to go home."

He looked over at her to see her reaction, but she was already looking at him when he did that, and that was super intimidating, so he pretended he just had to scratch his shoulder with his chin, or his chin with his shoulder, whatever.

"Fair enough," she said after a while. "What's on your mind?"

Bobert studied his hands, the calluses that had formed on them over the last couple of weeks. "I guess I was just wondering why you're taking part in an evil scheme. I know I'm just a kid and might not know, exactly, how the world works. But it definitely feels like an evil scheme to me, and I didn't think you were evil."

Now it was Imogene's turn to stare at her hands for a while. "I don't think in terms of good or evil. It's never really black-and-white like that. This is Nefaria. Most schemes have some evil to them—doesn't mean they don't do any good."

Bobert looked at her with less self-consciousness this time, giving her the look that his mom often described as the *come on, buddy* look.

"Fine, maybe it's an evil scheme. What's your point?"

"Well, just, everything I know about you, throughout your career you've always protected the kingdom. All your exploits have been for good. I've admired you my whole life, and I can't believe that . . ." He found his voice breaking, and he took a breath to try to steady himself. "I can't believe you'd be responsible for keeping me away from my family. That you'd put the kingdom you spent your life protecting in danger. That you'd make all these kids be a part of this guy's army."

On cue, Matt passed by them on the stairs. "Camila!" he shouted into the open air. "Is today a shampoo day or not? I forget, and I want to make sure my hair is looking its best tomorrow."

Camila squawked back something unintelligible, and Matt continued shouting while looking for her.

Imogene's gaze dropped to her feet, and Bobert sensed an opportunity. "I need something from the castle," he said. "There's a secret room that I think has the spell we need to break free—"

Suddenly, Imogene stood up. "I can't hear this. Not until I've been paid. You wanna try to sneak around, that's fine. And I'd be happy to help you once I've got what I came for. But until then, I'm sorry to say that I'm on the doofus's side."

Bobert reached out to her, desperate to make her stay. But he didn't want to tug at her pants or anything, so instead he just kept his hand outstretched in the air between them. She was walking away, and taking with her his only chance to break them free.

"Is this how you want to be remembered? After everything you've done for Nefaria? You want your legacy to be helping Matt, Blizzard of Lizards or whatever, become the king?"

Imogene paused at the top of the stairs. Her back was still to Bobert, but he held his breath, waiting for her to turn around and change her mind, to say she would help him. He didn't know what her payment was, didn't know how long she'd been dreaming about Grandma Gertrude's famous apple pie, how close she was to spending the rest of her life truly happy.

"Sorry, kid," she said, and entered the castle, leaving Bobert alone on the steps.

22

BOBERT SAT FROZEN ON THE STAIRS, looking out at the courtyard and all the kids resting there. So many of them seemed to have given up hope for escape, and maybe he should have too. There was definitely a feeling in his stomach that told him to give up, that he wasn't going to be able to do anything alone, so he might as well not try. What use was it having heroes if they disappointed you like that?

A few seconds later, Justin the cat came over and hissed at him, so Bobert stood up and made his way slowly back to Candelabra and Stanbert. He plopped himself down on the grass between them, and started yanking at the blades, ripping them up into little shreds, as if they were responsible for Imogene's rejection.

"What were you talking to her about?" Candelabra asked.

Bobert was momentarily surprised, as if forgetting that the conversation had happened in plain view of everyone. "Nothing," he said. "It was stupid."

"I don't believe you. No one goes up to talk to the bravest warrior in Nefaria if they think it's stupid."

"Don't tell me you were trying to come up with another plan and wanted her to help you with it," Jarrediah said, his eyes closed to the sun. It was on the mean side, but it was the least mean thing anyone other than Candelabra or Sylvinthia had said to Bobert since the failed barricade.

Bobert didn't say anything.

"What's he talking about?" Candelabra asked.

Bobert ripped out a few more blades of grass, not wanting to relive his terrible idea. He couldn't believe he was going to try another plan, one that would likely have gone just as badly. It was probably good that Imogene had shot him down.

"Bobert had this idea to keep Matt from coming back in," Sylvinthia said, picking at a scab on her forearm. "We tried it the day you showed up. It didn't go well."

Bobert looked around for something to hide in. Maybe he would dig himself a hole in the ground and bury himself, and that way he wouldn't have to live through the rest of the conversation.

Jarrediah chuckled from the ground, opening one eye and squinting at Bobert. "Oh my god, you really did have another plan." He shook his head. "Some people don't learn."

Bobert lowered his head, not wanting to look at anyone. Then he felt Candelabra touch his arm. "What's the plan?" she asked, her voice lowered. "Maybe we can help." After a few seconds passed and Bobert still hadn't said anything, she spoke again. "Don't listen to anyone else—just because they're too scared to try anything doesn't mean you should be too. Nefaria needs people who aren't afraid to stop evil."

A swell of emotion flooded Bobert's chest. He couldn't meet her eyes yet, but his chin wasn't almost touching his chest anymore. Candelabra was probably the bravest person he knew, he realized.

"You're only here because of me. So if there's any way I can help to get you out, I'm going to try it."

"It was my dare," Stanbert said, startling Bobert, who thought he was still napping. Apparently Candelabra had filled Stanbert in on the story of what had happened the day Bobert disappeared. "So I'm going to help too."

"Really?" Bobert asked.

"What else is there to do but try?" Candelabra asked.

Other than icing their bruises and tired muscles, they spent the rest of the afternoon figuring out the best way to thwart Matt without anyone getting caught. They had a lot of bad ideas, many of which required either superpowers or catapults that no one in the group had or knew how to build (and one of Stanbert's ideas needed thirty grapefruits, but they'd run out of those days ago). Despite how good it felt to have not only Candelabra and Stanbert on his side, but Sylvinthia and Jarrediah, too, Bobert was starting to believe that they weren't going to come up with a way out in time.

Until Bobert brought up the secret room.

Once he did, it was clear that *that* was the first step in the plan. And to get to the room again, they would need a distraction. But what kind of distraction?

Right on cue, Matt came out with his blasted wooden spoon and pot and started banging *again*, this time announcing dinner.

They all looked at one another at the same time. It was a great thing that Matt was such an annoying loudmouth.

"Okay, this is our chance," Candelabra said, saying what they were all thinking. "Bobert, go before anyone sees you. We'll give you the signal."

He nodded, and didn't waste any time saying something meaningful or expressing his gratitude to them. He just went. He kept his head low as he made his way across the courtyard toward the outhouses, not just to avoid eye contact with all those kids who blamed him for everything, but so that he wouldn't draw much attention from them. Now more than ever, being invisible would be good.

He reached the outhouses and pretended to stand in the three-person line. Then, after a moment, and before anyone else could line up behind him, he threw himself into the bushes that lined the nearby wall, not far from where Stanbert and Candelabra had landed when they broke in.

Meanwhile, Stanbert and Jarrediah rolled up their sweatshirts and shoes, Candelabra's bag, and a few armfuls of dried leaves that had blown into the courtyard from nearby trees, and stuffed them all inside Bobert's sleeping bag. They pulled out some of the sleeping bag's stuffing and rubbed it in the dirt, trying to make it look like Bobert's hair. It kind of worked, depending on whether or not parrots had super-good eyesight like eagles. No one was really sure if that was the case.

Right as they finished, Camila started making the rounds, flapping her way from Matt's shoulder and hovering by the kids. Camila looked down at Jarrediah and Stanbert and considered the sleeping bag next to them.

"He's pooped," Stanbert said, he hoped convincingly.

The other kids around the courtyard started gathering in the now-familiar dinner routine of lining up on one side for food and the other for drinks. (There were a bunch of sodas to choose from; unfortunately, they were all sodas that Matt himself had made as part of one of his failed evil schemes, which had involved creating a sugary-beverage-based conglomerate, and the flavors were things like pork chops, cream cheese, and burnt popcorn.)

During this hubbub, Candelabra and Sylvinthia tasked themselves with leading Matt as far away from the castle and keeping his back turned toward it. They maneuvered through the crowd lining up for food, and instead headed to where he was standing, still banging at his pot like a toddler entranced by the sound.

When he saw them coming, he put the wooden spoon inside the pot and reached into his robe and pulled out his wand, pointing it at them. "Careful, girls! You've seen my awesome power. Do not come closer, I'm warning you."

They both raised their hands instinctively and stopped in their tracks. Candelabra fought through the initial fear she felt and put on her sweetest smile. "That's what we wanted to say, actually! We wanted to thank you."

Matt lowered the wand a little and raised one bushy and erratic eyebrow at them. "Thank me, you say? Go on."

"Well," Sylvinthia said, taking Candelabra's lead, "we're just so thankful that because of you and Miss Petunias, we now know how to fight. A lot of our peers are still a little bitter about the whole being-captive thing, but Candy and I were talking about what a great opportunity this is!"

"Yeah. Who knows what we would have done with our childhoods if we were free, but we doubt it would be anything as cool as being part of an army that's going to take over Nefaria."

Now Matt lowered his wand and broke into a wide smile. "Ah, finally! Some of you fine young people have come to your senses." He looked over his shoulder at Imogene, who had just grabbed her food from the nearby table. "This is what I've been saying, haven't I? That they would thank me in the end." He let out a bellowing laugh, from deep in his belly.

Imogene watched the two girls intently, and both of them, sensing an intelligence much greater than Matt's, turned away and kept their eyes on the wizard, not wanting to get caught. "Whatever," Imogene said. "I'm taking my food to my room so I can pack. You're giving me that recipe tonight."

"Yes, yes," he said, waving his hand at her and turning his attention back to Candelabra and Sylvinthia. "Are you excited for our big day tomorrow, then?"

Candelabra grinned. This was going to be too easy. She tried not to look toward where she knew Bobert was right now, sneaking his way along the wall and approaching the castle. "Can we sit with you while we have our dinner? We'd love to hear more about the attack strategy, and all your plans for when you rule Nefaria."

"But of course!" He gestured with his hand. "Let's get you to the front of the line, shall we?" He led them toward the line, pushing kids out of the way. "I'll get you sodas. What would you like? Pickle? Cream of cat?"

Candelabra tried to control her gag reflex. "Um, I think there was an apple one? I'll do that."

As Matt turned to fetch the drinks, Candelabra tried to see where Bobert was. If he could get inside the castle before the speech even started, that would give him plenty of time to flip through the spell book and find the right page.

Before she could spot him, though, Matt returned, handing them their sodas. "All out of apple, I'm afraid. I hope you're okay with tree bark. Come, let us eat inside. We can discuss strategy in the comforts of my dining room."

"No!" Candelabra shouted. "Um . . . weren't you going to give your motivational speech during dinner?"

"I can easily give the speech after we've dined in comfort," Matt said, turning toward the castle.

"Well, I read an article about how kids are much more motivated by speeches *while* eating, not after," Sylvinthia said. Candelabra shot her a look, but Sylvinthia shrugged.

"Hmm, really? I suppose I should keep up on my academic journals. Been out of touch with the research and whatnot." He scratched at his chin, and a puff of dust flew up from his beard. Sylvinthia and Candelabra jumped back, trying to hide their disgust. "We could maybe bring everyone into the castle," he muttered. "The acoustics might be a little challenging, but . . ."

"What about the fountain?" Candelabra suggested. "We can sit and eat there while we wait for everyone to get their food, and then you can stand up in the middle and give your speech from there."

Matt turned to look at the fountain, as if just remembering

it was there. "Ah! A fine idea. Great visibility to all. A raised dais, almost—like a stage. Plenty of room for my signature extravagant hand gestures. Yes, the fountain it shall be!"

From a hiding spot in the bushes, slowly creeping along the wall, Bobert kept his eye on the girls, waiting for the right time to go. He also tried to be aware of Camila flying around, and of Justin the cat at the front door. He was still sleeping there, which didn't necessarily kill the plan, but Bobert didn't want to go in through a window. They hadn't tested them out, so there was no way of knowing if they were protected by spells, or if they might lead into a room that had since been locked.

Bobert waited patiently, watching everyone gather. Candelabra and Sylvinthia were eating with Matt at the fountain, nodding and pretending to be listening while he gestured wildly with his arms, almost hitting the girls several times.

Camila landed on Matt's shoulder then, possibly done making the rounds during dinner. Bobert stood as still as he could in the bushes, waiting for the right moment. It was kind of fitting, he felt, to be hiding. To not be seen, and in that way perhaps be able to bring things back to normal.

Soon Matt put his plate down on the ground and stood on the fountain. At first he was facing the castle directly. The sun had set and twilight was spreading across the sky, so maybe it'd be dark enough that Bobert could sneak by anyway? Or he would have to go to one of the side windows for sure. Then

Bobert saw Candelabra tug on Matt's sleeve and say something to him, and he adjusted and turned his back to the castle. Bobert sighed in relief.

Matt cleared his throat loudly. "Children!" he bellowed. "Gather round!"

No one moved.

"Come on," he said, his voice a little more pleading than authoritative. "Just, you know. Please?" He waved them closer.

A few kids obliged, but most did not. It seemed Matt would have to do with that.

"I speak to you tonight not just as your fearless leader, not just as your commander in chief, not just as Chillest Wizard, Master of Blizzards, not just as . . ." He trailed off. "I forgot where I was going with that. Ah yes!"

As he continued, Bobert saw Candelabra put both hands in her hair and shake vigorously, like she was shampooing. It was the signal they'd agreed on. Or some of Matt's beard dust had flown into her hair and she was trying to get it out. But Bobert was just going to have to assume it was the sign for him to *go*.

He looked at the front door to see if Justin was still there. And though he was, Bobert could see Jarrediah approach. The cat opened one eye as Jarrediah stepped toward him, not yet ready to pull himself out of the comfort of sleep. But another step forward and Justin reared up, arching his back, flattening his ears against his head, and hissing.

Jarrediah pulled out a little morsel of chicken that they'd been served with dinner and that he'd been saving as a snack. He beckoned the cat over, and Justin, suspicious but unable to resist, sauntered over to where Jarrediah was standing. As soon as Justin had taken the morsel into his mouth, he tried to run. However, the cat was old and hadn't done his post-sleep stretch routine. Plus, Jarrediah was tall, had gangly limbs, and—back before he'd been sucked into a gumball machine—had been one of the fastest kids in Nefaria. He scooped Justin up in his arms and pressed his face into his fur. "Good kitty!" he said. Justin started biting his forearm viciously, but Jarrediah held on.

"We will be marching not only through the kingdom, but through the history books as well! And when you have helped me achieve my dreams of domination, children, I will not forget you. You will have all the bubble gum you wish for; you will have . . ."

Now was Bobert's chance. He rustled his way out of the bushes and scurried to the castle wall, pressing himself flat against it. Then he sidestepped his way along the wall and toward the doors.

23

CANDELABRA MADE EYE CONTACT WITH BOBERT, who was almost to the doors of the castle. Opening the doors without notice would be the hardest part of the plan, and realizing that Bobert needed a little more cover, she tugged on the sleeve of Matt's robe.

"You're losing them," she whispered. "Go bigger. Louder."

"Bigger, you say?" Matt made a thinking noise, then smiled. "If I must!" He took a deep breath and screeched, "THEY SHALL KNOW OUR NAMES ACROSS ALL THE KINGDOMS, AND ACROSS ALL TIMES, AND ON MANY BULLETIN BOARDS! HISTORY WILL SCREAM ABOUT US!"

Bobert waited by the door, where he could stand in the shadows, away from the light of the torches. As soon as Matt started bellowing again, Bobert put his hand on the door handle and pulled.

The door moved with a bit of a groan. To Bobert it felt like the loudest noise he'd ever heard. He turned to look at Matt, cringing. But no one seemed to have noticed. He took a deep breath and inched the door forward more, keeping his eyes on the wizard. The door creaked, but Matt was shouting about how the town would throw them all a parade when this was all over.

After two more stomach-churning door nudges, Bobert had opened the door wide enough. He flattened himself as much as he could and slunk in. Once he turned and started to close it, a draft from inside the house—probably because of the broken windows—grabbed hold of the door and threatened to slam it.

Bobert stopped it just in time and shut it softly. He waited there for a moment, breathing through his nose, listening for the sound of Camila squawking or Justin hissing or Matt bellowing. And he absolutely was. But not about anyone sneaking into the house. Just his usual bellowing.

Once it felt safe, Bobert didn't want to waste any time. He rushed through what he remembered of the castle and made his way to the library. The secret passageway behind the bookcase was hidden again, but Bobert could see that same book, cleaner than all the rest, on that top shelf.

This time he didn't have Sylvinthia's height, though. He tried jumping a couple of times to reach it but couldn't quite get his fingers on it. So he looked around the room for something to help. The recliners seemed to be the best choice. They were a little far away, but if he could just push one close enough, then he could stand on it and easily reach the book.

When he lifted one of the recliners and tried to push it, it made a horrible scraping noise against the stone floors. What if someone heard, or noticed the scratch on the floor before the night was done? He looked around the room again and his sight landed on the little puppet stage. He ran over, hoping it wasn't bolted or glued to the floor in any way. It wasn't! And he could even carry it.

He wobbled over with it in his arms, and it was exactly the height he needed.

Bobert pulled on the book, and the bookcase moved out of the way again. Bobert took the stage back to where it was, and this time when he was in the stairwell, he slid the bookcase back so that it was almost shut. He left a space for his fingers to go in so that he could open it back up, but not so much that Matt or Camila would notice if they came in when he was still in the secret library.

Bobert scrambled down the stairs, switched on the lights, and ran straight to the book. It had been turned to a different page, this one a spell for how to get your cat to not bite you. Matt had clearly not gotten it to work yet.

But Bobert remembered the page number he needed, and he quickly flipped to it. A part of him thought that maybe he'd imagined the whole thing. That it was something his mind had made up during the last couple of weeks just to give him something to hope for. But no. He had remembered correctly. There it was in front of him: **SPELLS TO TRAP CHILDREN, TRAIN ARMIES, AND CONTROL OTHERS.** He scanned the page, looking for the words he really wanted to read. They weren't at the bottom of the page as he expected, so he flipped through to the next page. And the next.

His heart started to sink. All he saw were spells, and no information about how to undo them. He'd been silly to think that there would be instructions here for him. He didn't know anything about spells, didn't know anything about how magic really worked (aside from what he'd been taught in school, but everyone knew that the nitty-gritty science of magic wasn't covered until high school).

Then he saw it. Exactly what he needed.

HOW TO BREAK ANY SPELL IN THIS SECTION:

IT'S QUITE SIMPLE.

FIRST YOU MUST PLUCK A HAIR FROM THE
PERSON WHO CAST THE SPELL, EVEN IF IT IS
YOURSELF (ANY HAIR WILL DO).

THEN RECITE THE FOLLOWING WORDS:

Oopsie doopsie, undo this whoopsie.

NEXT, ONE OF THE ORIGINAL VICTIMS OF THE
SPELL (WHETHER THAT'S YOU OR SOMEONE
ELSE) WILL HAVE TO TIE THE HAIR INTO SIX-
TEEN KNOTS, UNDO FOUR OF THE KNOTS, RE-
CITE ANY POEM ABOUT MISTAKES, AND THEN
EAT THE HAIR, CHEWING EXACTLY THIRTEEN
TIMES.

**LAST, PULL THE HAIR OUT OF YOUR MOUTH
AND PINCH BETWEEN YOUR FINGERS, THEN
LOOK SOMEONE ELSE IN THE EYES AND SPEAK
WHAT YOU WANT MOST OUT LOUD TO THEM.**

WARNING: (SEE NEXT PAGE)

Bobert read the instructions two or three times. The warning on the next page made his stomach drop and his breath catch in his throat, but he'd worry about that later. He closed his eyes and tried to recite the instructions out loud to make sure he remembered. *"Pluck a hair, oopsie doopsie whoopsie, then I tie the hair into . . . um . . . sixteen knots . . ."*

As he was trying to remember what to do next, he heard applause coming from outside. Not a lot of it. Matt was done with his speech, yes. But it wasn't like all the kids were actually pumped up by it. Bobert guessed it was mostly Candelabra, Sylvinthia, Stanbert, and Jarrediah making all the noise in order to warn Bobert.

Bobert read the page another two or three times, then closed his eyes again to quiz himself. *"Pluck a hair, oopsie whoopsie doopsie, sixteen knots, minus four equals twelve, then a poem . . ."*

No, that wasn't it.

He tried again and again, but his brain couldn't seem to hang on to the order of the instructions. He might have kept trying until he got caught, but that was one good thing about

Matt's obnoxiously loud bellowing: Bobert could hear it all the way down in the secret library.

"Roll call!"

It was time to go. So Bobert did the only thing he could think of: he ripped the page out of the book.

He scrambled back upstairs and hopped out the first window he could find. Now that it was dark, he scurried through the bushes, then pretended to exit the outhouse area. He rejoined his friends right as Camila flew overhead, counting out loud to herself.

"Did you find it?" Candelabra asked.

Bobert could only nod, thrilled to have made his escape, but shaken by what he knew might happen when the spell was broken.

Imogene zipped up her bag. It hadn't taken her long at all to pack, and she'd known it wouldn't. But she was eager to get away from this place, to escape the memory of the last two weeks. While the kids were by no means all of a sudden lethal weapons, she had taught them how to maneuver in their ill-fitting armor, how to wield weapons. She'd taught them basic fighting tactics that would be useful in battle.

She found herself in the peculiar position of hoping that the wizard's evil scheme would actually work, that the king's army would lay their weapons down, unwilling to strike children. That, after all, was one of the codes of a warrior, and one she herself had followed throughout her years as one. But she didn't know if those codes stood up to an evil scheme quite like this one. If it came down to surrendering the kingdom or harming children, she knew how she would act. But she wasn't so sure about other knights, knights who might feel a little more loyalty to Nefaria than to codes of honor.

She waited in her room for Matt to come and bring her the recipe, so she could finally go. She'd originally planned to spend one more night and then start the walk back home in the morning, but now she didn't want to delay. She'd find an inn in town. This place was giving her the creeps, and the conversation with that kid was echoing in her head. How had she allowed herself to end up in this situation? Was a pie recipe really that important? And did she care more about her legacy than she'd thought?

She had to admit, the kid had had some guts to approach her like that.

An hour after she'd finished her dinner, Matt still hadn't come. Two hours later, he still hadn't come. So she went to find him upstairs in his turret.

He was sitting with his feet up on the windowsill, looking out at the starry sky and the scattered torchlights of the town below. He was drinking a cocktail of sorts, which was billowing with smoke and had a little umbrella in it.

"I've been waiting," Imogene said, announcing herself as she entered.

Matt was taking a sip and looked over the rim of his cup at her. "Me too, Miss Petunias! This day has been a long time coming. Please, join me for a toast to celebrate. This would not have been possible without you!" He gave a little push to a plate with a piece of toast on it, offering it to her.

Imogene had no time for pleasantries or toast. She went right up to him and knocked his feet off the windowsill. "The recipe. I trained your army. Now it's your time to live up to the deal."

Matt sprang forward, trying to sop up the bit of drink that had splashed onto his robes. "I just had this cleaned last month," he muttered.

"Come on, enough joking around. The recipe. Before I pull out my daggers."

This grabbed Matt's attention. But instead of reaching into his robes for a piece of paper or rising to some hidden spot in his room to fetch the recipe, Matt only smiled. "I'm afraid I can't do that, Miss Petunias. I never had it."

The floor threatened to drop out from beneath Imogene's feet. But she wasn't the kind to faint. She gathered the nausea and queasiness she felt and transferred it over to her muscles. Before Matt could move, she grabbed a fistful of his robe, pulled him completely off his chair, and shoved his face into the floor. "What did you just say?"

Matt chuckled, though it was clear she was hurting him. "I never had the recipe, Miss Petunias. I cheated you."

She pushed his face further into the floor. "What about the slice of pie I ate?"

"A simple enchantment, dear," he groaned as the stone floor cut into his cheek. "It was an average pie from the market. Below average, if we're being honest. But the spell tapped into your sense of taste, and your sense of nostalgia for the pie, and made you think that was what you were eating. It's a tricky spell to pull off, but I did pretty well, didn't I?"

Now Imogene let go, unable to replace her sadness with anger any longer. She slumped down onto the floor and put her head into her hands. "You never had it?"

Matt pulled himself up and went to an oval mirror on the wall to check his cheek. "No."

"But it's somewhere, right? You know where it is?"

Matt watched her through the mirror. "Unfortunately, no. All a big ruse. Everyone knows the recipe is lost."

"You'll pay for this," she said. Usually when she threatened someone, she meant it. But right now she couldn't muster the energy to rise to her feet. Which was all the time Matt needed to grab his wand from his drink-stained robe.

"No, I don't think I will. But I thank you for your service. When I rule the kingdom, I will send you all the pie you like."

Then he threw his head back and attempted his best evil laugh, but he broke out into a fit of coughing.

Imogene rose to her feet. She couldn't believe it. The rest of her days would be spent alone, without Grandma Gertrude's apple pie.

25

NIGHT PASSED IN NEFARIA the way it often did: on the brink of disaster, without most people knowing how close they were to life changing forever.

It was the first truly cold night of the season, and all around town, residents lit fires and huddled together in their homes, thankful for their families, or sick of them. The flying goats perched themselves on treetops, wrapping their wings around their bodies to protect against the chill. Monkey businesses shuttered for the evening, hopeful that Nefarians were coming to accept their entrepreneurial savvy as nothing more than that: a good sense for business. Ghosts roamed the halls looking for someone to chat with.

In every corner of the kingdom, scientists and witches, lords and duchesses, common folk, and a handful of animals—both common and noble—dreamed up new schemes. Schemes to bring them riches and schemes to bring them power, schemes that they truly thought would improve the lives of Nefarians for the better, and schemes they knew would only benefit a hand-ful of people and harm the rest. Schemes that were borderline evil and full-on evil, and many good schemes too. Schemes to make sure everyone in Nefaria had a roof over their head if that was how they liked to sleep. Schemes to feed everyone in Nefaria, whether the people being fed schemed for the good of others or not. Schemes to make sure that every living thing had the chance to live their life with the utmost dignity and happiness that could be externally provided.

And, yes, schemes to storm the king's castle. Schemes to shrink all the adults in Nefaria and let the children rule the land. Schemes to use wizard screens in order to hypnotize all the citizens of Nefaria into complacency and lethargy, and thus let other schemes run rampant. One certain cat who shall go unnamed schemed to poop in a certain unnamed wizard's hat.

The moon shone bright that night over the hills and valleys of Nefaria, with only the occasional cloud passing in front of it.

In the Bougainvillea household, Bobert's parents sat quietly by their fire like so many others. But it didn't seem to warm them at all. They kept looking at the small rocking chair in the corner of the room, imagining the child they could not remem-ber sitting there with them, maybe reading a book, if he was a reader. There were kids' books in his room, but they didn't like thinking too much about what that meant.

Elsewhere, Candelabra's sister looked out from her painting at the empty living room, wondering what time it was, how long it had been since she'd seen Candelabra. There was no way for her to know, what with the sun always shining in the blue sky.

Stanbert's parents felt the strong absence of their missing child, because they could remember him. The absence was so strong, in fact, that it felt like the only thing in the room. Like something loud and pointy and dangerous just sitting there with them, sucking up all the oxygen, making it hard to move, making it impossible to talk or think about anything else.

The Elders had approved a petition, and the king's army was going to be notified in the morning to conduct a formal search of Matt's castle. But morning felt so far away to Bobert's parents, and they wondered how they would manage to sleep that night, waiting for it to come. They wondered how Bobert was sleeping, hoping he had some measure of comfort and warmth, hoping that this was the last night he would have to spend at Matt's castle, forgotten.

And in the courtyard of that castle, Matt's weak warming spell failed to fully protect the children from the cold. They all shivered in their threadbare sleep sacks. Some had managed to fall asleep, maybe because sleep was the only way to fight off both the cold and their thoughts of what tomorrow would bring.

Bobert hadn't been so lucky. His thoughts were stuck in a loop. He was worried about what would come tomorrow at sunrise, when Matt would emerge with his wooden spoon and his pot and loudly proclaim the start of their march.

But he was also hopeful. Hopeful that Matt had not noticed and would not notice that a page had been torn from his spell book. Hopeful that he'd be able to pluck a hair from Matt's beard or matted mane and follow the rest of the instructions. Stanbert had even been able to remember a poem that was kind of about mistakes (it was about eating someone else's plums, which they all agreed counted).

Then his thoughts turned right back to worry, wondering if they would have to fight. Wondering if anyone would get hurt. Wondering how Sylvinthia and all the other kids who'd been stuck in the gumball machine a long time would react to how much Nefaria had changed while they were gone. Wondering if, once they broke the spell, Matt would just cast a new one over them. Wondering what would happen if this plan failed too.

The only thing he wasn't really worried about was the warning added onto the spell. The more he thought about it, the more he felt okay with the risk.

He tossed and turned, tightly holding the folded sheet of paper in his fist. And despite his raging thoughts and the cold, he managed to fall asleep, as if his body knew he would need the rest.

Morning came.

This time Bobert woke up by himself. The sun hadn't yet peeked out from behind the mountains, and Matt had yet to sound his annoying low-budget alarm. Bobert hadn't slept enough, and it was far too early to be up, but he felt ready, for once. The piece of paper was still in his clenched fist, and he opened it, reading the instructions over and over again. There was still a measure of queasiness in his stomach, but something had shifted overnight in his brain. His thoughts were no longer raging, wondering about what would happen or how. There were simply the instructions. There was simply the plan to ruin Matt's scheme and save the others. What came after that he would figure out later.

Breakfast was better than it had been their entire time at the castle. Instead of soggy, unflavored oatmeal, there was a whole bevy of delicious options to choose from. Pancakes stacked high and dripping with syrup. Sugary cereals galore. An omelet station manned by a magic-infused set of cooking utensils. Rice porridge and all the accompanying toppings one could dream of.

The kids feasted, forgetting for the moment their unfortunate circumstance, maybe even a little excited that they would finally leave the castle, finally see the Nefaria they'd been snatched away from. Many of them had secret hopes that they would be able to resist Matt's spell once they left the castle and just run home, if they still had a home.

Candelabra, meanwhile, decided to use her newfound closeness to Matt and offered herself up as the one to get a hair from him.

"Are you sure?" Bobert asked. "I can try. . . ."

"It's okay," she assured him. "He'll suspect less if it's me. I'll just go before I start eating, otherwise I might puke."

She went to say good morning to Matt as he did a terrible version of the calisthenic routine Imogene had taught them all. Then she pretended that there was something in his beard and she was helping him get it out.

"Owie!" Matt yelled out. Candelabra tried not to laugh at the sound of a grown man (especially one who was well over a hundred years old) saying that. Then she tried not to gag as she curled the hair around her finger and shoved it into her pocket.

"Got it," she said. "I think it was just some food or something."

She ran back to the group and presented the hair to Bobert.

"Ew," Sylvinthia and Stanbert both said at the same time. It was such a long hair, and it really did have some food traces on it. It also had a smell, which was pretty impressive for a single beard hair.

Bobert immediately went to the next step in the process.

He no longer had to read the words off the instructions; they'd burned themselves into his brain sometime throughout the night. "Oopsie doopsie, undo this whoopsie," he said, trying to imbue the sentence with meaning. He wasn't sure if that was necessary, but it felt like it wouldn't hurt.

"Wait," Candelabra said. "Wasn't there some kind of warning at the bottom?"

"We have no choice," Bobert said. He was already at work tying the knots. It was good that the hair was so long, because sixteen knots was a lot.

"Who should it be, though? I don't think it should be you."

But Bobert was too focused to answer. Or at least he made it seem that way. The gumball kids deserved to be free, and he definitely wasn't going to let Candelabra or Stanbert, the only people who had ever really seen him, be stuck with Matt forever. So he just kept working on the hair.

The first knot was easy. The second one too. Even the third knot was done in less than ten seconds. The ones after were trickier, but Bobert's fingers kept working quickly. No one wanted to say it, but it felt like this could really happen. Like they were going to break the curse before their march to the king's castle even began.

Then a shadow fell over them.

26

ALMOST AS SOON AS BOBERT NOTICED that it was Matt causing the shadow, he felt the paper getting ripped from his hands.

Bobert's heart leapt to his throat, and he dropped the semi-knotted hair onto the ground. He was then torn between keeping his eyes on Matt to see what he would do next and turning his attention to the ground to find the hair.

It turned out that the easiest decision to make was no decision, though, so he simply kept his eyes exactly where they were, unable to move. Because of that, he was able to see Matt's face the exact moment when he realized what the paper said. His cheeks reddened even more than usual, and some spittle formed on his lips as if by magic. Maybe it was magic.

"How *dare* you?" Matt screamed, turning his full attention to Bobert. "You conniving, sneaky, blasted, no-good . . . nincompoop!" He was so mad, his hat flew right off his head. "Yes, I said it. You nincompoop! You dare to attempt a coup?

Another mutiny? My whole plan could have been ruined! Years of planning. Decades!"

Bobert felt his body trying to make itself small. It was a reaction that felt like shame or embarrassment, but Bobert wasn't embarrassed at all. He was just sad he'd gotten caught, that *his* plan was now up in flames. He tried to fake shame in order to look at the ground and find the hair, but before he could, Matt reached down and grabbed him by his arms, pulling him up onto his feet.

"Hey, let go of him!" Candelabra shouted.

Matt whipped his head toward her. "You? I expect this from almost anyone else. But not you. I thought you were cool!" He held up a colorful thread of woven fabric. "I was coming over here to give you this, but I don't think you deserve a friendship bracelet anymore. You don't even deserve a friendship scrunchie," he huffed.

"Where are you taking him?" Stanbert called out. He rose to his feet to follow as Matt dragged Bobert toward the castle.

"None of your business!" Then, realizing that everyone was watching the exchange, he turned to the crowd. "Everyone, in your armor! Breakfast is over. We march in fifteen minutes."

Bobert looked back over his shoulder at his friends as he was getting dragged away. He didn't really care about the paper anymore. He'd had enough time with it. *The hair,* he mouthed as best as he could. *Find the hair.*

Candelabra watched him, feeling her heart sink. No, no, no. Not again. She noticed him mouthing some words at the last minute before Matt yanked him into the castle. Stanbert, however, was a pretty good lip-reader and immediately started searching the grass where Bobert had been sitting.

Once inside, Matt let go of Bobert and started pacing back and forth in front of him, muttering to himself. "The gall . . . can't believe . . . undo *my* spell? *My spell?* I don't think so." He went and stood in front of Bobert, fuming, his hands on his hips. "Well," he asked. "What do you have to say for yourself?"

Bobert said nothing. What could Matt possibly expect from him? It was better to just keep quiet.

But it seemed Matt knew that too. Before Bobert even had a chance to say anything, Matt pulled out his wand and said, "Hellicle jellicle, flippity floth. Turn this scoundrel into a sloth!"

The other captured kids did as they were told and started collecting their armor. They'd gotten much better at getting in and out of it over the past couple of weeks, and within minutes most of them were ready to go, almost eager to get out the door.

Meanwhile, Sylvinthia, Stanbert, Candelabra, and Jarrediah scoured the grass, searching for the hair. "We have to find it!" Candelabra urged.

"Maybe Bobert will be able to grab another one? I don't remember all the instructions, do you?" Stanbert said. He reached for something in the grass, but it was actually some goat fur that had fallen into the courtyard at some point.

The others' silence spoke volumes about how well they remembered the instructions.

"Uh," Jarrediah said. "You have to do math with the knots, right?"

"Does the poem come before or after the math?" Sylvinthia asked.

Stanbert knew they were outside, but it still felt like all the air had been sucked out of the room. They kept searching the grass, trying to play it cool when Camila flew by and squawked at them to get into their armor. Even when Sylvinthia shouted out that she had found the hair, holding it up for all to see, it felt like there was no point. They needed Bobert. And who knew what Matt was going to do to him?

Candelabra was the last one to get into her armor, which had been cobbled together from spare pieces that didn't fit anyone else. A lot of her was still exposed, since Matt had only counted on two hundred children for his army, not the extra two that Candelabra and Stanbert provided when they snuck in. Fortunately, Matt had never kept track of the kids, so he hadn't noticed that two of them had not been brought in by the gumball machine but had arrived on their own.

Candelabra couldn't bring herself to care about her insufficient armor, though. She was trying to count how many knots Bobert had tied in the hair, and looking nervously to the castle, waiting for him to come back out. Maybe Matt was just going to give him a good talking-to and Bobert would be allowed to join the rest of them.

Moments later, Matt burst through the front doors again, holding a little trumpet. He blew a vaguely militaristic bugle call. It reminded Candelabra of when her class had learned how to play the recorder in second grade.

"Soldiers! In formation, now!" he bellowed, sweating a little from his trumpet blowing.

There was a general rustle and clatter of metal as the kids lined up the way Imogene had taught them. It wasn't particularly fast or smooth, since they'd only been practicing for two weeks, not two years. But considering that most of them had fallen over and hurt themselves in their armor that first day, it was pretty impressive.

Because of where they were in the courtyard, Candelabra and the others lined up close to the front of the formation, which was meant to be twenty kids across and ten deep. The courtyard was a little too small to make that perfectly work, so it was kind of a squished formation that curled around the edges.

"Good enough for now," Matt grumbled. "Just, you know, spread out once we're outside." He scanned the crowd, muttering inaudibly to himself. Then he spotted Candelabra. "You! To the front. Yes, your friends, too. I want to keep my eye on you."

Candelabra was holding the hair in one hand and the bow she'd chosen as her weapon in the other. She had a quiver of arrows on her back, though there were only three of them in there. She'd shot a few over the courtyard wall when she was learning how to use it, and Matt had been too lazy to fetch them, either by magic or by feet. Now she glared at Matt as she and the others followed his orders and marched to the front.

"Good." He cleared his throat. "It seems that some of you weren't listening during the speech yesterday. Or at least you didn't listen to the implied portion of my speech. If all goes well, you won't have to fight for me. But I do expect you to follow my every command and not do anything that totally sucks, like this boy has. Now you can witness for yourself what happens when you toy with Matt, the greatest wizard of all time!" He laughed and then did a dramatic flurry as he looked to the door and pulled on a rope that led into the castle.

Nothing happened.

"Hold on," Matt said. "It'll take a second. You'll see why."

Still nothing happened.

"He's really ruining my dramatic reveal," Matt huffed.

Candelabra craned her neck to get a look at Bobert. But she couldn't see inside the castle. The crowd of children started to murmur. Matt, sensing that he was losing them, walked toward the castle. "There you are, you insubordinate swine!" He bent over, reaching down for something just beyond the door.

When he turned around, he was holding up the most adorable sloth Candelabra had ever seen (although every sloth was the most adorable sloth Candelabra had ever seen). But this one looked just like Bobert.

The crowd gasped, but they went "awww" at the same time.

"*This* is the plan he doesn't include us in? What a jerk! *I* want to be a sloth!" someone else yelled.

"No, no!" Matt shouted. "You don't want this! This is terrible! Look at him—he can barely move. And he certainly won't be running off to try to subvert my scheme. Let that be a lesson to all of you!"

A lot of the kids were still *aww*ing at Bobert's adorable new shape. And while Candelabra was just as taken by how cute her friend looked, another part of her was almost brought to tears. How were they going to break the curse now?

27

THE CITIZENS OF NEFARIA woke up feeling uneasy. Some because they'd been trapped in the quicksand pits the night before and had just barely managed to escape. Some because they'd been trapped in a painting for a year, with no sign that they'd ever be freed, and now their sister was missing. Some because they'd just gotten used to waking up feeling uneasy. It was the way of Nefaria. Some fresh devastation could be unleashed any day, and they knew it. Sentient noodles, or tax breaks for the only people who could afford not to have them—there was always something. Ghosts who'd just discovered knock-knock jokes and were desperate to try them out.

Others woke up uneasy because they'd been at the townhall meeting the night before when Jennizabeth finally gave her testimony. It had taken two weeks to approve her appearance at the Council, after which there was no longer any debate about an evil scheme being on the horizon. They wanted the king's army to go thwart the wizard already, rescue however many children he had with him. But the Council of Elders needed to approve the rescue, and apparently they never did that without having a ceremonial breakfast.

It was eight in the morning.

Bobert's parents had both woken up before sunrise. They lay in bed and pretended they'd be able to fall back asleep. Finally, they made some coffee, which they barely touched because of their nerves. And they waited. They looked out over the hills and valleys of Nefaria. They did not have a view of the town, but they knew that somewhere out there was Matt's castle, and that their son, whom they could not remember, was inside it. They wished they knew what they missed about him.

And just as they were having this thought, they heard a distant sound, made louder by its echoing off the mountains. They couldn't place it at first. If it had been winter already, they might have guessed an avalanche. If it had stormed recently, maybe it could have been a mudslide. It could have been a stampede, but this part of Nefaria didn't have the kinds of animals that typically stampeded, unless there was another scheme going on.

They both went outside and listened closely, barely breathing to avoid making any competing noise. Was—was that marching?

Imogene Petunias had woken up at a roadside inn, still enraged. She had considered seriously hurting Matt, but didn't want to get embroiled in any legal proceedings, not again. She'd had enough of those to last a lifetime. So she had stormed out, thinking that she could escape her rage by walking it off.

If that was the case, she had not yet walked far enough. Perhaps she would have to reach all the way home before she calmed down. Even then, it was possible she needed to fight someone. Hopefully a wizard, or someone who looked like Matt. She had dealt with many jerks throughout her life. But he was possibly the biggest.

She'd left her inn after quickly shoveling down her breakfast and was on the road leading away from town. Someone ran past her, going the other way. She barely noticed them. Then another two women ran by, each one trying to strap a scabbard onto her belt. Imogene would have warned them that that was a bad idea, that they should stand still to do that, but she was too slow. The shorter of the women tripped on her sword and fell, sprawling to the ground. Imogene stopped, meaning to go help. But the woman scrambled to her feet almost as soon as she had landed, and—as if she did not have the time to check herself for injuries—she continued running down the road toward town, simply holding her scabbard and sword in her arms as she did.

Imogene wondered what was happening. Then another five

or six people ran by. "There's an army!" a boy of sixteen or so yelled at her. "There's an army marching toward town!"

Right.

That.

Imogene watched the people rush in that direction, wondering how it would all unfold. But she was too angry to want to witness it all, too angry to be near Matt. She just wanted to be home. So she kept walking.

The Elders had dragged themselves into the meeting hall at dawn in order to file the special petition to the king. They spent the first fifteen minutes milling by the coffee machine, complaining about the fact that it was early. Then they spent fifteen minutes complaining that no one had made the coffee and drawing straws to decide who would have to. Elder Gusbus then threw a fit, claiming that the eldest Elder was exempt from coffee-making duties.

Once the coffee was made, they wasted time congratulating themselves for coming into the office so early, and for filing the special petition on behalf of the people. They were truly public servants, and everything they did was for Nefaria. They were proud of themselves, as well they should be

They were right in the middle of deciding what they would have for their ceremonial breakfast when they heard a rumbling in the distance.

There were also voices outside. People shouting. People running. The Elders shared a look.

"What's the procedure for going to look outside?" Elder Piñatacakes asked. "Do we need a quorum for that?"

Elder Gusbus rolled his eyes. "That's only during a public meeting."

When they finally stopped arguing and went outside to look, what they saw was dozens of people coming out of their doors, just like the committee was. Many more were running in the direction of the castle. There were occasional shouts of "Protect the king!" and "A scheme! Oh god, an evil scheme!"

The rumbling grew closer and closer. One of the Elders shrieked, and Gusbus would have turned and told them to keep their decorum in public, but he saw something approaching. A lot of somethings, actually.

They were clad in rusty armor and were bobbling their weapons. They were small, and definitely not the best marchers anyone had ever seen. But it was undeniable: an army, not the king's, was marching through Nefaria like it owned the place. And it was headed straight to the king's castle.

28

THE KING OF NEFARIA was a small and affable man who didn't necessarily understand the lives of those who lived under his rule. Oh, he had his advisors and what have you, people whose job it was to inform him what his subjects' lives were like, so that he could understand how his actions affected them. And he often went out to the courtyard for meet-and-greets, because he liked being seen as a man of the people. In a way he felt like he belonged to them. Granted, he didn't *really* want to get too close to many of those people. They didn't all smell great, and a lot of them had complaints about the kingdom. Which he found to be rude. *That* was what the Council of Elders was for. The king, they should have all known, was responsible only for the *good* parts of the kingdom. Anything bad was because of the Elders, or the people themselves, or sometimes the weather.

Anyway, it was hard to truly understand his subjects, no matter how much he tried. He had been born into his position, had been born into incredible wealth, and because of being royalty, he had been kept separate from all the others. So, no matter how many times he was briefed about his subjects, no matter how many tours he took to town or out to the countryside to say hello, there was no way he could truly understand their lives.

This was true even if, about thirty years earlier, he'd started feeling a deep sadness, like there was something missing. At first he felt guilty for feeling this unkingly way, but the royal doctors told him nobility did not exempt one from sadness. His wife felt it too, though they had long ago decided it was just a hole they would never fill. Maybe being rulers just wasn't that fulfilling. They focused their energies on running their kingdom, and their family.

Their children were always warm and well fed. They had never gotten trapped in quicksand or in gumball machines. The space around the castle was a strict no-fly zone, so they didn't even have to worry about getting pooped on by the flying goats. They didn't have to walk an hour to school (a royal tutor lived at the castle with them), and they certainly didn't have to worry about being invisible. They had grown old safely, and now lived in their own castles, with their own families.

Even though many evil schemes were aimed at taking away the king's rule, there were a lot of protections in place to keep him and his family safe. Because of this, the king could not really perceive certain things about the way other people lived their lives, the worries or concerns they had, and, yes, even the joys. He tried to. But he often failed, despite that sadness, which he felt made him more like the commoners.

That was why, when he looked out the window of his breakfast room and saw the huge crowd rushing toward the castle, he didn't immediately worry. This might have just been one of those things he didn't understand. People upset about the weather.

He stirred some milk into his breakfast tea and kept observing, curious, the way one observes an ant colony, perhaps. He rose from his seat and went toward the window, using the small stepping stool in order to get a good view. He wasn't sure why they kept it after the children had all grown. It had been in the castle for nearly as long as he'd been sad, and he liked using it even when he didn't need to.

At first, he wondered what it was that his army was doing out there. He hadn't approved any training exercises, and he hadn't even heard them leaving their barracks this morning. Which reminded him: he should really make sure to move the army barracks away from his bedroom window.

Then he looked closer and saw that the army was headed toward the castle, not away from it. And all the commoners who had gathered were rushing toward the front of the castle to stand in its way.

"Hmm," he said out loud, even though he was alone in the breakfast room.

Then the alarm started ringing throughout the castle.

The king jumped, his tea splashing everywhere, just as Geoffiffer, his most trusted and favorite advisor, burst into the room, her trusty clipboard tucked under her arm. She noticed the spilled tea, the way she noticed everything, and grabbed a napkin from the table. She handed it to him as she held him by the arm and led him out of the room. "Please sir, come with me. Nothing to panic about, just a possible invasion, milord."

"Oh dear. Been a while since one of those. A serious one?"

"It appears so. We'll have to take you to the safe room." They were already out of the breakfast room and headed down the hall to the stairs.

"And my wife?"

"She's been evacuated and is safely off the premises."

"Okay, good. I want to meet with General Silverlocks. And will someone bring me a puzzle down to the safe room? It gets so boring."

He scratched his forehead, right below where his crown rested. The sweat there always made his skin itchy.

Bobert struggled to keep up with the marching, and Matt just kept tugging at the leash around his neck, as if that would make him move any faster. It was as if the wizard had had no idea what a sloth was when he'd turned Bobert into one.

Bobert felt sluggish and sleepy. The world looked different since he'd been turned, and it was a little strange to look down at his body and see all that fur, the sharp claws. But he hadn't had a whole lot of time to process the change before they'd started marching.

Candelabra offered to pick Bobert up and carry him while they marched to the king's castle, but Matt scoffed. "So you can conspire against me again? Ha, no, thank you!"

"But I'll be trampled," Bobert said in his new slow, deep voice.

So Matt allowed a different boy—one who was having quite a tough time lugging his battle ax—to carry Bobert on his shoulder instead, as long as he marched near Matt.

Now they were about to enter the town square. Bobert was facing the wrong way, but thankfully he could turn his neck almost the whole way around to face the front. His six long claws were incredibly strong, and gripped the space between the boy's chest and shoulder armor plates.

Bobert couldn't believe it had been just over two weeks since he'd been in the town square. Since he'd put that nefickle into the machine and set off this whole thing.

It was a very different sight now from what it had been that night. At first he couldn't tell what exactly was happening. Why were so many people here so early in the morning, and why was there so much yelling? Why were they rushing toward the castle?

Then he realized that they were trying to protect the castle. From him.

Well, maybe not from him specifically. He'd caught his reflection in some of the shinier armor around him, and in a few store windows, and boy was he cute. Cute and not very dangerous-looking, those claws notwithstanding. Even in their panic and fear, Bobert could hear some of the townspeople go "aww!" at seeing him. He definitely wouldn't have been invisible at school if he had been a sloth.

The people not focused on Bobert were focused on the fact that there was an army invading the town. They probably couldn't tell that the army was made up of children who'd gone missing over years and years, children who'd been forgotten. They probably couldn't tell that they were under the spell of the loudmouthed wizard at the front of the battalion.

But a very short encroaching army was still an encroaching army.

A few of the kids cried as they advanced. The spell stayed strong, along with the training and practice they'd received from Imogene. Together they marched, steadfast, toward the castle. Not perfectly together—Imogene was good but couldn't work miracles. Instead of the satisfyingly rhythmic stomping of a good army march, they sounded more like a bull crashing through a cymbal stall at the market.

Bobert spotted Mr. Barracooties, the shoe repairman that Bobert's family always used. He was holding a pitchfork and a torch (even though it was sunny out) and standing in front of his store.

"Mr. Barracooties!" Bobert yelled, waving at him. Or, rather, *trying* to wave at him. By the time he'd let go with one arm and started moving it in a direction, the marching army had passed the store. "It's me! Bobert!"

If Mr. Barracooties heard him, he didn't react. The army kept marching on. It occurred to Bobert that some of the kids might not be crying because of their inability to run away. He thought of Sylvinthia, how she'd said she didn't know how long she'd been gone for. Forget two weeks—this was the first time the others had been in town for years. Decades. And no one had remembered them this whole time.

The realization made Bobert so angry and sad that even his cute sloth face wasn't smiling anymore. Matt was truly evil, and he had to be stopped.

"Attack us!" Bobert shouted. "He's counting on you to not fight back! You need to stop us!"

But Bobert was speaking too slowly, and the army was marching on. The only one who seemed to have heard him was Matt, who turned while marching and gave Bobert a single, taunting wink.

29

BOBERT KEPT YELLING at the familiar faces he passed, but he couldn't get the words out fast enough. "Attack us!" he tried shouting. "Don't let us through without a fight! We're actually very bad at it!"

A few of the other kids around him got the gist of what he was going for, but they were still angry at him, still wanted to blame him for their current circumstances. Only once Candelabra, Stanbert, Sylvinthia, and Jarrediah started yelling alongside him did those calls start to spread to the others. Sylvinthia especially was yelling at the top of her lungs: "Don't you remember me?"

They had no choice but to march, but they didn't have to do it quietly. At least for a little while.

The army was almost at the entrance to the royal castle. The only obstacles that stood between them and the entrance were a moat, a raised drawbridge, and about three hundred loyal Nefarians.

"Keep yelling!" Bob said. "Don't give up!"

Matt turned back to face him again, rolling his eyes. "Come on! I'm standing right here. You think I can't hear you? That I won't try to stop your silly little plan?" Without waiting for a response, Matt reached into his robe, pulled out his trusty wand, and flourished it at his army, at which point they all fell silent.

Bobert tried to keep yelling, but he couldn't scream, or shout, or even make that weird croaking noise that vocal cords sometimes make. His voice was gone.

No sounds came from his cute little sloth mouth, nor from his friends' still-moving normal human mouths.

Now Matt lifted his arm in a fist and the army behind him stopped marching.

The townspeople watched nervously, wondering how this was supposed to work. Did one of *them* have to speak first? How would they choose who would speak? Where were the Elders? It should have been one of them. Could the Elders at least have a quick meeting to help them decide? And why was this army so short? Had they been created that size specifically to attack their enemies' shins? Because that was genius. Hopefully someone from the actual king's army would come out of the castle soon to start negotiations with this scientist in his pajamas, or whoever was leading the army.

"Good people of Nefaria!" Matt shouted. "Many of you no

doubt know already who I am."

He paused and scanned the crowd for recognition. The people gathered there turned to look at one another and shrugged. "Is that you, Gary?" someone shouted.

Matt groaned. "No!" He swung his robes about him in dramatic fashion. "I am the great wizard Matt, of course! Mattholomew, Whose Power Is Matched by Few? Chillest Wizard . . ." He waved a hand at the audience as if they'd done something wrong. "You know what? It doesn't matter. You will all know me soon enough. As your ruler!" He paused again. The crowd just continued staring at him. "Or as your king, perhaps. Master? I'm still toying with what my official title will be." He twisted his beard into a braid, getting lost in thought before snapping out of it.

"Either way! Tremble before me and my mighty army. We shall make our way through you one way or another. We shall enter the king's castle, and we shall likewise dispose of His Royal Army. I'm happy to give you this one opportunity to lay your weapons down."

"Never!" Fredonia, the town butcher, shouted. She gripped her turkey carcass—an odd choice of weapon, no doubt—harder.

"If you surrender, we will not strike," Matt assured them. "Lay your weapons down and stand aside, and this will all be over quickly."

"No," Taylor the typist (not to be confused with Tyler the tailor) cried out. "This is our kingdom, and we like the king. He's all right! We will not let you just storm in without a fight."

Matt smiled. There were more people joining the crowd standing between his army and the castle. Something about that made Matt already feel successful. *Look at all these people*, Matt thought. *Here for him.*

"Yes, I thought that might be your stance," he said to the crowd. "Before I set my highly trained army on you, I'd like to show you something." He turned to his army of silently crying and teeth-chattering children (it was still quite cold).

Matt waved his hand, and all the kids found their arms involuntarily moving toward their helmets to pull them off.

The townsfolk gasped.

All those who had been at the town hall meeting had a moment of enlightenment. "Oh . . . ," they all went, piecing together what had happened from what they were seeing. There was a lot of snapping of fingers and adults saying to one another, "Had you figured it out? I totally hadn't figured it out." They chatted about that for a few moments until it really dawned on them that if they were going to try to protect the kingdom, they were going to have to fight children.

Matt watched this with great pleasure—the kind of pleasure that came to a man whose evil scheme was playing out exactly how he had envisioned. Plus or minus a few dozen years and some pretty major tweaks to the plan. But whatever! It was really happening.

Bobert, on the other hand, watched this realization with great dread, not that his face showed it. He couldn't really control his cute sloth smile. That was just his face now. He couldn't bring himself to look at Candelabra, or Stanbert, or Sylvinthia, or Jarrediah. He had failed to free them. He had failed everyone.

The other kids, most of them, were starting to become numb to it all. The gumball machine had been one thing. They'd mourned the loss of their previous lives and become used to what it was within that weird dimension. They'd gotten used to the gumball smell and the gumball taste and the gumball sound of everything. The way time didn't seem to move.

Then there was Bobert's arrival, the first in so many years. And the sudden move to Matt's castle. The brief hope of freedom. And then falling into a new routine. This morning, for the past few weeks, had felt like something to look forward to. The last step, perhaps, before they could reunite with their families, their friends. Their pets. The lives they used to have.

But this march into town had changed all that. They'd seen how much Nefaria had transformed while they'd been gone, and it dawned on them that years really had passed. So many years that they didn't recognize some of the buildings, didn't recognize the way people dressed, didn't recognize any of the people. What was worse, no one seemed to recognize them.

They'd been truly forgotten.

So, whether or not the mob of townspeople looking at them laid down their weapons didn't matter, did it? What would they do if they weren't in Matt's army? Where would they go?

Bobert saw this shift on the faces of those around him, and his heart broke in a way it never had before, not even when people ignored him.

The air hung heavy between the villagers and Matt's army. They were all waiting. Not to see what would happen, because it seemed clear to everyone what was going to happen. They were all just waiting for *when*. Surely, any minute now, the drawbridge would be lowered, and the true protectors of the kingdom would come rushing out.

But then what? Would the king's army fight children?

Finally, one person stepped toward Matt. It was Tyler, the tailor.

He looked Matt in the eyes, defiant. Matt smiled and cocked his head, as if daring him to try something.

"These children are innocent," Tyler proclaimed. "We will not strike them, and they will not strike us. This is not a battle; it is an attempt at a bloodless coup." He turned his back on Matt and the children to speak to the other townspeople. "We must just stand our ground, and he will be left with no choice but to turn around!"

Just as the townspeople were about to cheer in response, Matt waved his wand in the air. As he did so, Candelabra stepped out of line, holding the shovel that she'd chosen as her weapon. She didn't want to do it, and she shut her eyes hard, as if not seeing the world would be enough to keep her body from following Matt's invisible orders.

But it wasn't.

Matt waved his arm again, and Candelabra swung the shovel, hitting Tyler square in the back and knocking him over onto the ground.

30

"THE KINGDOM IS AT STAKE!" General Silverlocks yelled. "We must do anything we can to protect it!"

"We will not start striking down children in the street!" Geoffiffer shouted back, getting more flustered than the king had ever seen her.

"So you would have them strike *us* down?"

"They're tiny—how much could it hurt?"

The king sighed as his advisors argued on, and he ambled over to the window to look out at the scene below. He could see both inside the castle walls—where his army was gathering by the front gate—and outside, where the invaders had stopped their march.

Some of the townspeople were gathered on either side of the army, but some were scurrying away, especially those with children, as if afraid that their kids might get absorbed into the tiny battalion. The king scanned the faces of his subjects. He didn't recognize any individual person—of course not, the kingdom was big and he met many people—but he could spot their fear. Part of him wished he could go down there and hug them, if not solve the whole issue in one fell swoop. But that was what his advisors were for.

Next he watched the faces of the opposing army. They seemed pretty scared too. Well, the sloth didn't. The sloth just looked cute. He made a mental note to tell Geoffiffer he wanted to adopt one after all this was over.

Not far from the sloth was a girl with two long braids poking out from her helmet. He didn't know why his eyes lingered on her. She didn't look particularly afraid, at least from what he could tell from the castle window. She looked frustrated, and a little sad. Suddenly the king felt a swell of determination.

He turned to his advisors and spoke over them. "If we start harming children in the name of the kingdom, the kingdom is worth nothing." Geoffiffer stuck her tongue out at General Silverlocks.

"Then we cannot lower the drawbridge," General Silverlocks growled. "Let them amuse themselves."

"Are you out of your mind, man?" the king grumbled, his eyes glued to the girl with the braids. "There are innocent children out there at the whim of a mad wizard in a filthy robe that frankly does not suit his complexion! We must go rescue them at once."

"But sir! Then we could lose the kingdom."

"And if we allow this to happen, the kingdom is already lost," the king shot back.

Outside, Matt was getting more irritated at the long wait. He had already gotten the townspeople to not only lay down their weapons but move out of the way. The situation felt doomed to them, or at the very least out of their hands. The king would have to decide.

And that was basically his job as a king.

Having lost the argument, General Silverlocks approached the knight in charge of the drawbridge. Then, in barely a whisper, knowing what it would mean, he said what the king had ordered him to do: "Lower the drawbridge."

Bobert watched in silent desperation as the drawbridge began to crank downward. He had stopped trying to scream at his fellow townspeople, stopped trying to make arm motions to get them to stop, to fight. Now he just wanted to get Candelabra's attention. He wanted to know if they'd found the hair. He wanted to free the other kids before it was too late.

This whole time he'd been repeating the instructions to himself so that he wouldn't forget the way to break the spell. Right now it would be impossible to do it, because none of them could speak to recite the poem. Not that it mattered without the hair. If they hadn't found it, they needed to get a new one from Matt. Which really shouldn't be too hard, what with how much he had and how often it fell out. Even from a few yards behind Matt, still clinging to the armor of the boy who was carrying him, Bobert could see at least three silvery hairs on Matt's robe.

He reached his long sloth arm out to try to tap Candelabra's arm, but she was out of reach, and the boy carrying him wasn't helping at all, oblivious to what Bobert wanted. So Bobert let go of the armor and climbed over to the person in front of him. He hadn't even realized that it was Stanbert until he had swung across the gap between the two boys and tumbled over Stanbert's shoulder and onto his chest.

Stanbert looked sad, but he still managed to smile at Bobert. *Hey,* he mouthed.

Bobert returned the sad smile, and they turned their attention to the drawbridge again, even as both of them were scanning the crowd for their parents. It was a slow drawbridge.

Bobert now tapped Candelabra on the shoulder. He was surprised to see her crying silently. She felt so guilty for what she'd done to Tyler. She knew it wasn't her fault, that it had been her body acting through Matt's magic. But it had still been her body. And Tyler had been knocked out for a few terrifying seconds during which she thought she'd killed him.

He'd been helped to his feet by those around him, after which the crowd began to part. They all knew that Tyler was lucky to have been struck by a shovel and not a sword or an ax, of which there were many in the child-sized army. Even after that, none of them would strike the children. So they stepped aside and decided that the king's army would know how to handle it.

And now that the drawbridge was about to touch down, they waited with bated breath for the ensuing battle. They didn't even know what to hope for. Would the knights be able to disarm the children somehow? Or would they have no choice but to strike them down? To actually fight? And did they even want to live in the kind of kingdom that struck down children to keep someone in power?

Finally, they heard the thud of the wooden drawbridge hitting the grass on the other side of the moat. Inside the castle, the king's army was gathered in their armor, and in perfect formation, all of them able to carry their weapons properly. General Silverlocks, who everyone in the kingdom knew was kind of a jerk but a good strategist, stood at the very front, wearing the feathery cap that marked him as a general.

Without waiting to see what the general would do, Matt waved his arm, motioning for the children to follow him. They began marching.

General Silverlocks, not to be outdone by a silly wizard and a bunch of children, motioned for the knights behind him to start marching too.

The drawbridge wasn't all that long, so the anticipation felt by everyone involved didn't last. The two armies stopped once again, this time in the middle of the drawbridge.

Matt and the general both tried speaking at the same time, trying to be the first to do so in order to assert their dominance over the other. Neither one stopped—they both kept going with the speeches they'd planned in their heads. Someone from the crowd yelled, "One at a time!"

"General," Matt bellowed, nice and loud, so that the crowd could hear he'd gone first. "Stand your army down! Or we will be forced to strike."

"No! *You* do that," the general shouted back. "We are the king's army, the mightiest army in Nefaria and many other kingdoms too. Your army is clearly untrained and outnumbered."

"Nuh-uh!" Matt shouted.

The general huffed. "Look, that soldier right there is maybe eight years old. How much training could she possibly have? And she's holding that ax backward! Plus, count your army and then count my army. And this isn't even all of them. You can't argue with numbers."

"Of course I can! I can argue with anything I want," Matt said, running a hand through his beard and fluffing it out in some weird display of manliness or something. Bobert definitely couldn't tell what he was going for. "Anyway, our training and our numbers don't matter. We're willing to strike. Are you?"

Without waiting for the general to answer, Matt motioned for the children to put their helmets back on. The crowd held its breath. Bobert clung tightly to Stanbert, bracing for the swords to come down on them.

The kids began marching again.

General Silverlocks unsheathed his sword.

The kids got closer.

Nefaria held its breath.

The knights . . . moved. Not toward the children. Not with their weapons drawn. But aside.

They parted, forming an aisle straight into the king's castle. A few of them laid down their swords, and then the rest followed suit. Even General Silverlocks.

The whole town watched as Matt and his army of children marched into the royal castle to claim the throne.

31

GLOOM AND DOOM ARRIVED in Nefaria.

An evil scheme had worked, and Matt the wizard was ruling over the land.

None of the residents of Nefaria had any idea what to expect. Their whole world could change on the whim of one very silly madman.

One would think that someone who spent so many years dreaming of taking control of the throne would have many specific ideas of what to do with that newfound power. But sometimes the thirst for power is shortsighted. It wants only the power itself, not necessarily what the power wields. So far, he had only decreed that wizards were first-class citizens and everyone else had fewer rights.

"Okay," Geoffiffer said. She was not politically appointed and stayed on as an advisor no matter who was king. "What rights do non-wizards no longer have?"

Matt waved his hand in the air. "Oh, I don't know. Parking."

"Parking, sir?"

"Yes! Revoke all non-wizard parking permits." He laughed and then coughed because he still wasn't good at his evil laugh.

"Anything else?"

He scratched his beard for a while. "Where are we on the parade? It's okay if you're planning a surprise one. I don't want to know. But I definitely do want a parade," he said.

Geoffiffer took a deep breath. "Okay, sure."

"And I want everyone there! There don't have to be any chants or anything, but if people want to, maybe something like 'Matt, Matt, he's the best ruler we could ever ask for! We love him so much, and actually want to be friends, not just loyal subjects.'"

"You don't want the chant to rhyme? Something short and catchy, maybe?"

"It was just a pitch," he mumbled.

Geoffiffer excused herself with a sigh, and Matt looked over at Camila, who was perched on the throne. "Don't give me that look. I'm being a great king/ruler/master of Nefaria. And yes, I still think that title works best with all the slashes in there."

"Whatever you say!" Camila squawked.

"'Whatever you say,'" Matt repeated in a high-pitched, mocking voice. He picked at some lint on his robes and flicked it. It caught the attention of Justin, who batted at it briefly, then looked up at Matt.

"What are you looking at?" Matt huffed. "I'm bored too."

For the past week he'd been celebrating, making changes in the décor of the royal castle, ordering advisors on meaningless errands (most of which involved fetching food). He flaunted his victory by holding evening speeches projected on wizard screens all over the land, which people watched out of some sort of emotional masochism. Even other wizards tuned in only to mumble about how he was giving them a bad name.

When it came to ruling the land, Matt didn't really have any ideas. He sent someone to his castle to collect his three finger-guns portraits and hung them up in the (actually) great hall. He made General Silverlocks cook all his meals for him. (A silly choice, really. The general was a terrible cook, and the royal cooking staff was right there, just twiddling their thumbs, unable to tell the general that no, that wasn't thyme, and anyway, thyme was not the ideal herb for the dish he was putting together.) Matt sent the royal army home without their weapons, but kept the king locked up in his safe room, along with a certain troublesome sloth.

It was perhaps the smartest move Matt had made after capturing the castle, because it kept Bobert separated from Candelabra, who still had the hair, but couldn't remember the instructions to undo the spell. Bobert *could* remember. He remembered so well, in fact, that he had trouble thinking about almost anything else. But he didn't have the hair.

The rest of the gumball kids were mostly allowed to roam throughout the castle's compound. It was a much nicer compound than Matt's, and significantly larger. Not to mention: it wasn't a gumball machine. So a lot of the kids, especially those who had felt a sense of pride and allegiance to Matt that day of the march into town, felt grateful. They felt like life was better this way. They were still under Matt's spell, and unable to leave the castle, unable to truly be free. But it was a greater freedom than they'd known before. There was no training. The food was better than Matt's soggy sandwiches (not *much* better, thanks to General Silverlocks, but still). Being happy in the castle also meant not having to think about the years they had lost. If they focused on being happy about being part of the monarchy, then it meant they didn't have to think about the family members who had lived on, not remembering them.

In the king's safe room, where he'd been locked up, Bobert reached for a puzzle piece. It took him a while.

No matter how slowly his new body moved, his brain had not stopped racing since he'd been placed in the room. Had his parents seen him? Would they have recognized him—if they even remembered him? Did the gumball kids blame him again, and were Candelabra, Sylvinthia, and the others now joining in on hating Bobert? What kind of havoc had Matt unleashed on Nefaria?

He had been planning incessantly how to get back to

Candelabra, how to break Matt's spell, how to save Nefaria. Or just how to get home. He missed home, missed his dad's goat stew, missed his room and his books.

He asked the king about every nook and cranny of the castle, every hidden passageway, every secret door.

Unfortunately, the king seemed kind of bummed and just answered with one or two unhelpful words. He had always depended on others to lead him around the castle, so he wasn't very familiar with the hallways. He did say that there was a secret way in and out of the safe room via an underground tunnel, but that it had collapsed after a recent earthquake, and they hadn't gotten around to fixing it yet.

There was a friendly ghost who came to visit them often. She looked like his grandma, with curlers still in her hair and an old-fashioned dress with a frilly collar. Her name was Mrs. Shavingham and she'd been alive two hundred years ago, and had all sorts of questions for Bobert about life as it was now. Unfortunately, she had so many questions for him that she never answered *his* questions before she floated through the walls looking for someone else to talk to.

Every now and then Matt came down to gloat to Bobert and the king. But there was something empty about his taunting, something a little desperate for a response, which neither of them ever gave him. It felt to Bobert like the wizard was lonely, which almost made him feel bad for him. Loneliness was hard.

Other than those interruptions, Bobert thought about escape. But the only option Bobert had was to get out through the main door, which Matt kept locked and guarded by both a knight and a gumball kid at all times.

But what use was that? He had tried—again and again—to help. To be brave. He was done trying. It seemed like he simply didn't have it in him.

Bobert placed the puzzle piece in the spot he'd thought it belonged, but found it didn't fit. He sighed slowly and moved the piece back to the pile he'd pulled it from. It took twenty minutes or so. The whole time, Bobert kept thinking: *Oopsie doopsie, undo this whoopsie, then you eat the hair, then . . .*

Candelabra, Sylvinthia, and Stanbert stood on the parapet walk of the castle, looking out at the quiet town. Everyone was dressed in black, most of them glancing over at the royal castle with what must have been deep sadness in their eyes (even though the kids were a little too far to tell for sure).

Candelabra was a shell of herself, worried about her sister not knowing where she was. She'd thrown some paper airplanes down below to get word to Sandraliere, but she couldn't be sure anyone had passed them along. Matt was still keeping the kids under a spell that prevented them from leaving the castle.

Sylvinthia had been especially quiet and sad. She wandered the halls almost like she knew them, like she was a ghost haunting the castle. A sad ghost who liked to run her fingers along the walls and stare up at portraits of the royal family for hours.

"What are we going to do?" Stanbert asked, for the millionth time in the last few days.

No one bothered answering him. They had run out of ideas, had talked about every possible plan. Nothing had worked so far, and they were starting to think nothing ever would. Candelabra pulled the hair out of her pocket again, counting the knots one more time, as if that would help her remember any of the rest of the instructions.

They knew there was a poem about mistakes involved, but as the days had gone on and they'd tried to remind themselves of the different steps, they'd only succeeded in confusing themselves further. They needed to get to Bobert to break the spell. But everything they'd tried—pretending to be waiters bringing food for the king; storming the doors; lighting a fire so that the guards would have to step away from the door—had backfired.

There was no use. They were going to be stuck inside that castle forever.

Beyond the castle walls, the town was in a state of shock. The people who'd stood in front of Matt's army to protect the kingdom, only to step aside and let him through, had not been able to sleep at all. They didn't know what else they could have done, but they still had their regrets.

The parents of Nefaria—even those whose children were still safe at home—gathered every day to discuss their options. Though they still couldn't remember Bobert, his parents had a whole house full of evidence that he had been in their lives. They had looked at the books on his shelf, studied his toys, and pieced together the child he was, and they were excited to be able to get to know him again, even if they never remembered what had come before.

Other parents were not going to mourn or grieve: they knew their children were alive and well. But the march into the castle had been a reminder of Nefaria's constantly lurking evil, and it had served as a lesson in fighting battles preemptively, before your kid was gone from their room and your memory.

They had felt the briefest glimmer of hope and joy before the kids disappeared into the castle. After that, Matt had ordered the drawbridge to come back up, and the kids had not been seen again, except when occasionally peeking out from a window, or pacing back and forth on the parapet walk.

Stanbert's parents had tried to contact him on his wizard tablet, but either the reception wasn't great, or Matt had placed a firewall—a spell to make Nefarianet signals catch on fire—to keep the signal out.

The Elders themselves were at a loss as to how to proceed.

They were beholden to the king, who now was Matt the evil wizard. But he had only made that one decree, and he hadn't even filed the proper paperwork with it. To be honest, they weren't even sure if the same paperwork was needed anymore, or what the proper procedure was. For anything!

So the Elders mostly stood around hemming and hawing and saying things like "Point of order!" Meanwhile, Bobert's parents watched the proceedings with blank expressions. They'd been on a roller coaster of emotions the last few days, and now exhaustion threatened to make them fall asleep in their chairs.

When the army—and their presumed son—disappeared into the royal castle, Mr. and Mrs. Bougainvillea at first tried to think of what else they could do. Could they contact wizards to see if any of them could break the spell? What about mercenaries to see if there was anyone who could storm the castle without fighting the children? The moat was protected by sharks with lasers strapped to their heads, so they couldn't swim across themselves, but maybe someone could.

All that fizzled out after about an hour, though. There was no fighting, no violence, and no one was in imminent danger. The crowd dispersed, hungry for lunch, starved of anything interesting to see. A few of the knights had stuck around waiting for orders, but General Silverlocks was staring blankly at the castle, also needing to be told what to do.

The kids were inside, yes. But there was a new king now. Life was going to be different, whether or not they stood there all day. So they looked at one another, not needing to say out loud the phrase that adults in Nefaria had often said, that day and many times before: "We can't do anything about it."

Imogene had made it back home. She poured herself a cup of coffee and went out onto her deck, next to the fire, which she built high and raging to combat the colder days. She sank into her favorite chair and put her feet up on the banister, picking up her book from the side table next to her.

But the coffee didn't taste as strong as she would have liked, or as rich. It tasted burnt. And no matter how many times she started over at the top of the page of her book, not a single word of what she read sank into her brain.

News had reached her about what had happened in town. And she had been trying to convince herself for days now that she didn't care. That she had been cheated just as much as the rest of Nefaria. But no matter how many times she tried to shake those thoughts and return to her book, none of it felt right.

At first she thought maybe it was the pie, or the lack of it. The fact that her hope had been broken after all this time.

When Imogene's parents had died in a terrible banana-peel incident, her trader uncle had taken custody of her and brought her on the road with him. One day, when she was not much older than Bobert and many of the kids trapped in with Matt, she and her uncle went to Grandma Gertrude's apple-pie shop, in one of the far corners of Nefaria, almost on the border of the kingdom of Infamia. Imogene's world changed forever. Grandma Gertrude's was not just the perfect apple pie. It was a pie that could heal. For the first time since she'd been orphaned, Imogene had felt strong enough to carry on.

Her uncle's schedule made it impossible to return to Grandma Gertrude's often, but they went twice, and both times she'd eaten the pie, Imogene had felt like there was true goodness in the world. Like it wasn't all just fighting off evil to keep a different evil in power. Some things were inherently good and worth protecting.

That was, of course, before Grandma Gertrude died, taking the recipe with her. Imogene had kept traveling with her uncle, practicing her battle skills to help fight off highway robbers and the various evil schemes they inevitably encountered on the road. But she'd never stopped thinking about Grandma Gertrude's pie, about the joy she had felt when eating it.

Now that she knew her original dream of retirement was over, she realized that she actually wasn't that sad about the pie itself. Something else was bothering her. Something about what that kid had said to her could not be forgotten, no matter how much she tried.

Imogene closed her book and put it back on the table beside her, looking out at the hills and valleys below, wondering when she would be able to enjoy them the way she wanted to.

32

BOBERT WASN'T INVISIBLE anymore. There wasn't even anyone around to see him or not see him. He was alone in a way he never truly had been before.

Which was a shame, because in his current sloth form, he probably would have been more popular than he'd ever had a chance to be.

But that wasn't what mattered to him. He missed his parents. He missed his daily walks to and from school. Missed, even, being in class, taking notes, and looking longingly at the other kids joking together, passing notes. He would give anything to feel left out like that again.

Maybe it was easy to think that way because he had a feeling that he would never have to. That, if they were free, Candelabra and Stanbert would pass notes to him, that they would meet him after school to walk into town together (no visits to gumball machines, though). And that was what hurt Bobert the most. That he could see the life he'd been longing for, the friends he'd been craving for so long. But he was stuck in this safe room with a despondent king who had stopped doing anything but putting puzzles together.

Three times a day, a guard would come in with food for the king and leaves for Bobert, even though his new digestive system worked pretty slowly and he didn't get hungry that often. Bobert tried making a run for it a few times, but even if he hid by the door and waited for the guard to come in, he never made it more than two steps beyond the doorway before the guard would pick him up and place him back inside.

The only comfort Bobert had was the fact that he had still not forgotten the instructions to break the spell. Quite the opposite. He'd repeated them to himself so often that they felt permanently etched into his brain. He had even written his own poem about mistakes (he didn't have to think very long or hard to get enough inspiration), and had prepared to say what he wanted most out loud to the world. That part was pretty easy too.

Without a hair from Matt, though, it was useless. And no matter how many times he'd combed the floor of the safe room, or scanned the clothes or armor of the various guards who came by, he hadn't found anything.

Well, that wasn't strictly true. He had found a hair one time, though it was more of a blond color than a gray. He'd done the whole spiel, and it hadn't worked, so it probably was someone else's hair.

It was seeming more and more like this would be Bobert's life.

Until the wall started shaking.

Bobert felt his little heart racing. He raised his head toward the sound as quickly as he could. The king, meanwhile, grumbled about his puzzle table rattling as a few pieces fell to the floor.

"What is that?" Bobert asked in his slow way.

The king merely shrugged.

Bobert climbed down from the floor lamp he was using as a perch and started crawling toward the wall. "Isn't this where the secret tunnel was?"

The king glanced at the wall. "Hmm," he said, which wasn't a helpful answer at all.

Now things quieted down. Bobert kept approaching the wall, trying to listen more carefully. Maybe it had been another earthquake, he thought, like the kind that had caused the secret tunnel to collapse in the first place. Or maybe some sort of animal was rooting around to make a home. He was pretty sure the room they were in was technically underground.

After another moment of silence, Bobert was about to turn back around and maybe help the king with the puzzle, when there was a thump at the wall. Then another. "Where's the entrance?" Bobert asked.

But he didn't need to wait for the king's answer. The wall he was staring at suddenly came crumbling down.

There was a big cloud of dust and dirt, which caused the king to cough. Bobert wasn't sure what would emerge from the new hole in the wall. He assumed it was bad news, though. Some new trick of Matt's, some new evil scheme that would make everything worse than it already was.

He wasn't expecting anything good to come of this. And he certainly wasn't expecting to see Imogene Petunias.

She was holding a shovel, and was dressed in full battle regalia.

Imogene waved her free hand in front of her face, trying to clear some of the dust from the air. When it had all settled, she surveyed the room she was in. She'd known the king was going to be in there, and that had been her goal. She hadn't known to expect a sloth, though. The sloth blinked back at her, looking equally surprised to see her.

"Miss Petunias!" Bobert said.

Imogene looked toward the king, but he was working on a puzzle and had barely seemed to notice her dramatic entrance. There was no one else in the room, so Imogene looked back down at the sloth. Who, it seemed, was waving at her.

"You're one of the kids?"

Bobert nodded slowly.

"Okay," she said. "Let's get you and the king out of here. Your Highness? Will you follow me, please?"

"Can I bring my puzzle?"

"We'll come back for it," Imogene said. She leaned down to carry Bobert into her arms.

"Where are we going?" the king asked. He seemed like he kind of wanted to stay in his safe room and keep putting the puzzle together. Sadness touches people in different ways.

"Getting you to safety," Imogene told the king.

"Wait," Bobert said, though he had to repeat it a few times, because Imogene had walked over to the king and was trying to help him to his feet. "Wait!"

She paused. "What?"

"You came back." He almost hiccupped, the words suddenly heavy in his throat, even though he felt lighter. "You think Nefaria's worth saving. You think we're worth saving."

He could swear he saw a smile tug at her lips before she rolled her eyes. "No time for speeches, kid. Let's go." She gently removed a puzzle piece from the king's hands and pulled him up to his feet.

"We can't go yet," Bobert said, swallowing his emotions for now.

"Why not?"

"We have to find my friends."

Imogene was leading them toward the hole in the wall

already, clearly impatient while waiting for Bobert to finish his sentences. "Don't worry, we'll come back for them."

"No!" Bobert shouted, as best as he could. "Now. I know how to break the spell. If we try to come back later, and they notice the king is gone, Matt will just go out with the child army that no one will fight anyway."

Imogene groaned for a second; then she seemed to really look at Bobert. "Wait, do I know you?"

He nodded. Speaking really tired him out. Most things tired him out in his current form. "I was the one who asked you to help me—"

"Okay, okay." Imogene interrupted, running a hand through her hair. "I get it. If we wait for you to say everything you want to again, we'll be here all day."

"Did either of you see my blankie?" The king asked. "I'd rather not go without it. And I know it was around here somewhere."

Imogene rolled her eyes, then shifted Bobert so that he was on her back, his strong arms wrapped around her neck. "New plan, Your Highness. You can finish your puzzle."

"Yippee," the king said, without much enthusiasm in his voice.

She turned to look at Bobert, whose head was poking out over her right shoulder. "Do you know where your friends are?"

Bobert shook his head.

"Okay, so, what *is* our plan?" Imogene asked. Bobert couldn't believe that the greatest living warrior in Nefaria was asking him what to do. And that he had an answer. "Try to explain it in as few words as possible," she added, interrupting him before he could get started (which was pretty easy to do). "I want to have some time left in my retirement when this is all over."

Bobert smiled. His regular smile, not his sloth smile.

"Step one: Lure the guards inside."

Imogene returned the smile. "I'm surprised that the wall tumbling down didn't do it, but I appreciate you being succinct. I think I can handle that."

Still carrying Bobert on her back, Imogene walked over and knocked on the door loudly. Then she shouted, "Oh my god! The king is trying to escape!"

There was some chattering on the other side of the door. "What? How?" the adult guard said.

"Hurry! Before he gets away!"

Soon Bobert could hear keys jangling, and the door was pushed open. An adult guard in armor walked in, followed by one of Matt's newfound child loyalists, who was prodding the adult guard with a large stick. "Don't let him get away!" the kid yelled.

Once they were inside, Imogene tossed Bobert onto the kid and yelled, "Hug his face!"

Bobert did as he was told, holding on with his incredible grip to the back of the kid's head. The kid started shouting straight into Bobert's fur, which tickled. Meanwhile, Imogene grabbed the guard's helmet and turned it around so that the visor was facing the wrong way. The guard stumbled about, shouting. Then Imogene grabbed the keys away from the knight, picked up Bobert from the kid's face, and marched them both out the door, shutting it behind her.

"What about the king?" Bobert asked as Imogene locked the door.

"He'll be fine. What's step two?"

33

CANDELABRA, SYLVINTHIA, AND STANBERT had met at their usual spot on the parapet walk, to try to look out into town and spot their families (although Candelabra knew hers wouldn't be there). Sylvinthia still didn't want to know what year it was, and though she never talked much about her parents, she seemed to be very hopeful that they would be outside the castle one of these days. When they'd failed to spot anyone they knew (town was pretty close, but the distance of the moat and the height of the parapet made it hard to make out any faces on the people below), they started what had become their routine: searching the castle for Bobert, or a way out, and preferably both.

There were many, many rooms in the royal castle. Far more than there had been at Matt's, which made sense. They still hadn't explored all of them, especially all the libraries. Unlike Matt's, they were stocked full of all kinds of books, not just weird magic ones. Sylvinthia had told them about the secret library at Matt's, and they became convinced that there had to be one like that in this castle too. So they checked every single book on the shelf to see if it would open up a secret passageway.

So far, none had. But they weren't going to give up.

"Let's turn left here," Candelabra said, looking at the map of the castle she'd drawn on a sheet of paper. She wasn't as skilled as Sandraliere, but she thought the map looked pretty good.

They came upon the royal sauna. Which was pretty cool. Well, not cool. It was warm and muggy. But it was just a cool thing that the castle had one. "I've never been allowed here before," Sylvinthia said, then quickly corrected herself. "None of us have, I guess."

After feeling their way around the steam to make sure Bobert wasn't hiding in there somewhere, they turned back around.

"Have we checked the roof?" Stanbert asked. "Maybe he's on the roof."

"I don't think castles technically have roofs," Sylvinthia said. "At least this one doesn't. Or is the parapet where we were earlier the roof?"

"Let's just keep following my map," Candelabra said. "It'll be hard to keep track of everything if we go out of order."

They were in a weird part of the castle. It was surprisingly quiet. Maybe because they'd gone to one of the lower levels, and it was dark and damp. There were a lot of kids milling about the castle, trying to keep themselves entertained. Some had posted up in the kitchen, partially to make sure they never went without food, and partially because they'd gone without good food for so long, and it was amazing to be near a well-stocked pantry and icebox. Even if the kitchen staff weren't being utilized to their proper skill level. There were all sorts of frozen meats, and spices from many kingdoms they hadn't even heard of before.

Other kids had made themselves at home in certain bedrooms, claiming them for themselves. But the kids mostly stuck to the prettier, sunnier parts of the castle, it seemed. The knights of the king's army who had been left inside sometimes roamed the halls too, those who had decided that they would honor Matt's rule. Most of them, though, stayed in the barracks and played card games to pass the time.

All of a sudden, Candelabra heard footsteps. She shushed the others as they walked down the hallway. She didn't want to run into any of Matt's new suck-ups and have them go tattle that they were snooping around. As had become a habit for her, she stuck her hand in her pocket to feel for Matt's hair.

It was still there. She breathed a sigh of relief, and when she heard the footsteps head in another direction, she motioned for the others to follow her into a doorway to the right.

Imogene and Bobert had heard voices coming down the hall, and since step two was staying hidden until they could find Candelabra, they decided to go in another direction. Imogene scrambled back, her footsteps surprisingly light and quiet. She found a set of stairs that led up, and even though that was likely to lead to more people, they didn't have much of a choice.

"Do you have a particular plan for how to find your friends?" Imogene asked. "Or do we have to search the entire castle?"

Bobert shrugged, letting the silly sloth smile—which spread across his face even when he wasn't trying to smile—speak for itself.

"Great," Imogene said.

Matt was sitting on the king's throne, popping grapes into his mouth. For the first few days, he had made Camila and Justin do it for him. But then they got sick of it and told him he could do it himself.

So that's what he was doing.

"Life as a king is good," he grumbled out loud, hoping that ghost lady might hear him and come by to ask her forty or fifty questions.

If he was being honest, life as a king was a little boring. There weren't as many people to hang out with as he'd imagined. Maybe after the surprise parade came together there'd be more visitors to entertain. He was sure people were waiting until after the parade to come pay him a visit. He tossed a grape high in the air, opening his mouth to catch it. It landed somewhere near Justin's bed on the other side of the room.

"Ahem," Geoffiffer said. She had been hoping that she might be able to guide Matt to do slightly less evil things than if he were left on his own. However, she had found that he didn't do many things in general.

"Did you see that one?" Matt said, chewing on a new grape he quickly pulled from the bowl. "I tossed that one so high. A new record, I dare say!"

Geoffiffer didn't think it was worth pointing out that she had seen him grab it. "Sir," she said, clearing her throat again. "I wondered if Your Highness has any particular plans today. Any orders you might like to hand out?"

Matt tossed another grape up, which hit him in the nose and then rolled down his robes and onto the floor, coming to a stop right by Justin's nose. Justin sniffed at it and then went back to sleep. "Oh, sure!" Matt proclaimed. "Yes, I have many orders to hand out. Plenty of plans for my kingdom!"

"Wonderful," Geoffiffer said calmly. "Such as?"

"Um." Matt ate another grape to buy himself some time. He knew that he was supposed to be scheming. That that was the whole point of an evil scheme. Not just to achieve power, but to continue to do evil things with that power. The problem was that he had thought this would all be . . . better. And the disappointment was making scheming much harder.

"I was thinking . . ."

"Yes?"

"That perhaps . . ."

"Go on, sir. . . ."

"Well, as you know. The goats! And I hear of monkey business. A lot of monkey business going on. Too much monkey business, is what I hear."

Geoffiffer could tell what he was doing. "Mm-hmm?"

"Well . . ." Matt popped another grape in his mouth, chewing slowly and thoughtfully. He was saved, though, by an urgent knock at his door. He sat up, excited by the development. "Enter!" he bellowed.

A guard walked in, his helmet turned around. A child was with him, crying, with fur stuck to his lip. A second guard walked in behind them, leading them by their respective shoulders. "Sir," the second guard said. "I found these two in the king's safe room."

"*I* am the king!" Matt roared.

"Yes, right. What I mean to say, is I found them like this in the former king's safe room."

Matt suddenly realized what was happening. "Is the king gone?"

"No," the guard said. "He was doing a puzzle and might not have noticed the breakout attempt."

Matt sat back in his throne and tossed another grape. This one hit him in the eye, but he pretended it hadn't. "What's the problem then?"

Now it was the crying child who spoke up. "It was Miss Petunias! She took the new kid."

Matt dropped all his grapes. Camila flew off his shoulder and snagged a couple for herself. "Sound the alarms," Matt said, feeling an unexpected lightness in his stomach. This wasn't the adoration he had expected when he took the throne, but at least someone cared enough to defy him.

"Um, we don't have alarms," Geoffiffer said. "We have the castle crier, who makes the announcements."

"Well, then have him call all the knights to attention. I need all hands on deck! And feet! Everyone in armor. We must root out these—"

Normally, Geoffiffer would never interrupt a monarch. But she had learned quickly that Matt needed to be interrupted or he could go on very long rants. "Sir, you sent the castle crier home early after your takeover. You said you didn't like his face."

"Oh, that's right. I did not. Those eyebrows." He shuddered, and then his sense of urgency returned. He might not have worried if it had been a bunch of townsfolk who'd made their way into the castle, looking to rescue the kids. His spell was still active, and still very effective. Every now and then he made the children do silly things like bark or flap their arms just to prove it. But Imogene Petunias was a different story.

Imogene Petunias made him nervous.

THE ROOM CANDELABRA HAD LED SYLVINTHIA and Stanbert into turned out to be an art studio. Which was fun and all—and included some rather pretty landscape paintings, which made Candelabra wonder if the king liked to paint, or if some of the knights had taken to entertaining themselves this way—but it became clear quickly that it included neither the king nor Bobert. They waited for a moment to make sure the footsteps they'd heard in the hall had passed, and then Candelabra creaked open the door again.

As soon as she did, two familiar sounds came rushing in at them. The first was a loud banging that gave them all flashbacks to those horrible mornings in Matt's courtyard. It was even the exact same pitch. "Did he really bring that dented old pot here?" Sylvinthia groaned. "Why would he do that? They have pots and pans here!"

The second familiar sound was Camila's squawking. "Intruder! Intruder! Everyone on alert! All soldiers, juvenile or otherwise, are to report to the courtyard! Intruder!"

Imogene and Bobert, meanwhile, had slipped into a linen closet. They'd made it up the flight of stairs when the racket started and kids started running around everywhere. They, too, heard Camila squawking about an intruder.

"What do we do?" Bobert asked. "We'll get caught before we find them."

"This might be the perfect thing for us, actually. He's making them gather in the courtyard. Which means everyone will be there, including your friends." She looked at Bobert, making out his expression in the dark.

"And?"

"We know where they'll be," she said. "We don't have to scour the whole castle for them. We just have to sit tight and then find a way to get their attention, so they can bring the hair to us."

They waited for the noise outside the linen closet to quiet down. Once it felt like the coast was clear, Imogene creaked the door open and carried Bobert out into the hall. "Which way?" she asked him.

Bobert shrugged as best as he could, to save the time it

would take him to tell her he had been stuck in that room the whole time and didn't know anything about the castle. Imogene sighed.

Fortunately, Matt hadn't thought to keep lookouts or sentries posted anywhere. So, Imogene explained to Bobert, all they had to do was find a way up to the parapet, where they would be able to look into the courtyard.

Once the hubbub settled down, that was exactly what they did. For a moment, as they searched, Bobert couldn't believe he was a sloth riding on the great Imogene Petunias's shoulders through the royal castle trying to free his friends and two hundred other children from an evil wizard's scheme. So much had changed in a few weeks.

"You okay back there, kid?" Imogene asked, interrupting his thoughts.

"Yes," Bobert said, and when Imogene turned to look over her shoulder at him, he could have sworn she almost looked impressed, though he didn't know why.

There were a ton of hallways and doors that led to all sorts of rooms. Some weren't really useful to them, though Bobert was certainly curious (especially about the room full of plants, which looked particularly tasty to him).

Once they found the right staircase, they emerged out into the parapet. Bobert couldn't help but turn his face to the sun and close his eyes. How great it felt to be out in the fresh air again, to be out in the world.

Imogene crouched down so they wouldn't be spotted and got close to the barrier wall facing into the courtyard. It was a mess of armor and moving bodies down there. "Can you spot your friends?" she asked Bobert.

"Um, I can't really see great," Bobert said, starting to wave a hand in front of his face, though he knew it would take too long for that test to work. "I think sloths have bad eyesight."

Imogene rolled her eyes and tried to remember who Bobert's friends had been during training.

Down in the courtyard, Matt was yelling instructions that few were really listening to. He was saying he would do a bunch more evil things if Bobert and Imogene weren't found immediately, but it was clear that he couldn't think of anything evil to threaten them all with. His loyal followers were trying to take attendance, even though no one had come up with an official list of everyone in the castle.

This was very helpful for Stanbert, Sylvinthia, and Candelabra, who at that moment were not in the courtyard with everyone else, but rather leaving their hiding spot. When they'd heard the "alarm" ring out, they'd scurried back into the art studio and pretended to be statues. It was a terrible idea, but no one came looking for them, so they got away with it.

Now they had had the same idea Bobert and Imogene had had, and were trying to find a vantage point to look down at the courtyard to try to spot Bobert. However, Sylvinthia seemed to have a perfect map in her head of the castle, so they avoided a similar exercise of opening doors and taking incorrect staircases.

Which meant that only a few minutes later, as Bobert tried to blink away his day blindness and Imogene scanned the crowd of children, the friends were reunited.

Candelabra had always been the fastest among them, but even if that hadn't been the case, she would have run fastest to Bobert. He was safe. He was still a sloth, but he was safe. And he was with Imogene Petunias.

"Stay low!" Imogene hissed.

As soon as Candelabra was with Imogene and Bobert, she held out her arms. "May I?" she asked.

Bobert couldn't tell right away what Candelabra was asking for. Could she . . . borrow Imogene's sword? Could she run away from this castle and never come back?

Then he noticed she was looking at him, and he pieced together that the arms-out approach, if he were still in human form, would be asking for a hug.

Overjoyed, and a little dazed, Bobert climbed out of

Imogene's arms and into Candelabra's. By the time he did, Stanbert and Sylvinthia were there too, and they all huddled around Bobert in a group hug. It was such a relief to be reunited that Bobert almost forgot that their mission wasn't over.

He only remembered when a shout came from below. "There's someone up there!"

The group froze. They stared down at the army below, who stared right back at them. One of the kids, still wearing his cobbled-together armor, was pointing up at them, while all the other knights looked like they'd frozen in place. For a second it seemed that no one knew what to do. Then Matt, standing in the middle of the courtyard, took in a deep breath, his cheeks getting red with anger, spittle flying everywhere. "Get them!" He flourished his wand.

"Nuts," Imogene said.

She turned to Bobert. "Now would be a good time to do whatever you have to do to break the spell."

Bobert whipped his head to Candelabra. Well, not really. Again, sloths move really slowly. By the time he was looking at her again, she had answered the question he was going to ask by holding up the hair she'd hung onto this whole time.

"Do you remember the steps?" Sylvinthia asked, her voice pleading.

Bobert nodded.

The castle was starting to rumble again as dozens of people in armor began making their way toward the various staircases.

"First—" Bobert started to say, but Imogene interrupted by grabbing the hair from Candelabra's hands and putting it in his claws.

"No time for you to explain. You have to do it. We'll hold them off as long as we can."

Bobert looked at the silver and somehow still-smelly hair in his paws, then back up. Everyone was eyeing him. He didn't know if he could, didn't know if it should be him at all doing this. But then he made eye contact with Candelabra, and she didn't even have to say anything for him to know that she believed in him, that she could see his fears and his doubts, and that she knew he could do it anyway.

Then Imogene knelt down and looked at him directly. "Kid, you've got this. You've been so brave throughout all of this. Just keep going."

Bobert nodded, and looked down at the hair in his claws. "There's just one more thing you should know," he said as he worked. "The warning."

"What did it say?" Stanbert asked.

"It's a curse on whoever breaks his spell," Bobert said. "It could get stuck onto me forever. I could be under his control forever. And you would all forget me."

"What?" Candelabra shouted. "Then stop!"

Bobert shook his head. "No time," he said, and he was glad it was true, because he didn't want anyone to try to argue with him. The other kids who'd been stuck in the machine had already suffered a long time. They deserved to be remembered, to be free.

"Oopsie doopsie, undo this whoopsie," he started, as quickly as he could. And he started tying the hair into the required remaining knots.

"Bobert, no," Candelabra said, tears in her eyes.

The others, meanwhile, looked to Imogene for guidance.

"Stand in a circle around the little guy," she said, starting to stretch to prepare. "The kids are still terrible warriors—no offense—so just try to push them over. They'll fall on their backs and won't be able to get up because of the weight of the armor. As for the adults . . ." She trailed off. "Well, hopefully they still feel weird about attacking kids."

That was when Imogene noticed Matt point his wand at them. "Shoot," she said, but it was mostly for effect. She was already grabbing at the dagger tucked into her waistband. Before Matt could finish commanding the kids, she whipped it down to the courtyard. Retirement had not affected her skills; the wand burst out of his hand, falling to the ground in two pieces.

"Curses!" Matt shouted, bending over to pick it up.

"That should buy us some time," Imogene told the kids.

"But they're still coming after us." They could hear the walls of the stairwell nearby reverberating with clanking armor, heavy footsteps, and yelling.

Candelabra, Sylvinthia, and Stanbert joined Imogene in some stretches, all three of them looking at Bobert and starting to cry, but not knowing what else to do.

Bobert looked up at them. He wanted to focus on the knots, but if he was going to be forgotten, he wanted them to know it was going to happen. He wanted them to know that it was okay with him.

"What?" Candelabra said, looking from the stairway back to Bobert, her eyes wide.

"It's okay," he said calmly. "It's worth it. I'm used to being forgotten. We weren't friends before I got cursed here. So I'm used to being alone. But before you forget me, you should know: me, your sister. Neither one was your fault. You're not to blame for someone else's evil."

Bobert had just finished tying the knots when the first knight emerged from the stairway, interrupting any response Candelabra may have had. Bobert begged his body to move quicker, but it was no use. Fortunately, Imogene kicked the knight in the chest, and he went tumbling down the stairs, taking a bunch of others with him.

"Bobert, we're not gonna let you do it," Stanbert said, but some Matt loyalists were starting to emerge from another staircase at the opposite side of the parapet.

"One of you go try to push them down the stairs!" Imogene yelled.

Letting out a groan of frustration that she couldn't think of another solution that didn't involve Bobert cursing himself, Candelabra ran off in that direction, but by the time she got there, they were already flooding out. She kicked one man in the shins, since he wasn't wearing his full armor. He hopped around on one foot, yelling "Ouchie!" One girl she recognized as being very loyal to Matt came at Candelabra with some nun-chucks, but fortunately another adult was running beside the girl and the nunchucks hit him instead. Candelabra decided she had to retreat, and went running back to the group, rejoining the circle around Bobert.

"How's it going?"

Bobert knew he didn't have the time to answer. Instead he moved on to the poem. "I have eaten the plums . . . ," he began. It started just like Stanbert's poem, but was about some other plums.

The army was moving in quickly, from both staircases now. For some reason they weren't running toward the group, just marching, maybe because Matt hadn't bothered trying to teach them how to run. Still, they were moving in closer, swords and other weapons at the ready.

"Hurry up!" Stanbert yelled. They all turned to look at him, and then turned pointedly toward Bobert. "Right," he said. "Sorry. But they're coming closer!"

Bobert finished reciting the poem and, with the cutest wince ever seen, popped the hair into his mouth and began chewing the required thirteen times.

The group moved in a tighter circle around Bobert, protecting him from the mob of guards and children coming at him. They were approaching from all sides, some of them even climbing up the sides of the castle walls to reach them. It felt like a zombie horde coming at them (even though only Sylvinthia had lived through an actual zombie horde, back before she got stuck in the machine).

Camila now flew over the castle wall and shrieked, baring her talons and coming straight for Bobert. At the last moment, though, Stanbert curved his body over Bobert to protect him. Camila dug her talons into his shoulder, causing him to scream out in pain. Candelabra, who had been using her shield to ward off the kids coming from her side, dropped it so she could grab the bird and wrestle it free from Stanbert.

"Let go of me!" Camila squawked.

Candelabra wasn't about to do that. Instead she grabbed the bird with both hands and stuck her out in front of her face, trying to ward off the attacks coming her way. The nunchuck girl was back and swinging them in wide circles, and those looked like they hurt a lot.

"Nine!" Bobert announced out loud.

"Chew faster!" Stanbert yelled. He had stood back up and was linking arms with Sylvinthia, wincing from the claw wounds in his shoulder. But there were simply too many kids, and they were starting to grab hold of the protective circle around Bobert. Imogene was trying as hard as she could to keep the children from breaking through their line of defense. She was moving so fast it seemed like she had at least four arms. Bobert wished he had more arms.

"If you give up right now, I will let your punishment be swift and not quite as painful as it would otherwise be!" Matt had appeared on the far side of the parapet, behind the horde of children who were coming after Bobert. He waved his broken wand continuously, trying in vain to get the little sloth boy to stop. How didn't all of these children see the wonderful gift he'd given them all in bringing them with him to the castle to rule. "You can live as part of the ruling class! But only if you stop this tomfoolery! You cannot break this spell. I'm too good a wizard."

"Twelve," Bobert said.

Two tall boys had grabbed hold of Stanbert and were pulling him, creating a hole in the circle. Two other girls were right behind, reaching in to try to grab on to Bobert. He laid himself down flat against the ground, flatter than he'd realized he could get. He didn't want to give them anything to hang on to.

"Miss Petunias!" Matt said, growing more desperate with each second that Bobert wasn't in his control. "Stop this right now and I will cast a spell on you. Every pie you ever taste will be Grandma Gertrude's famous apple pie! Who cares if it's real or not? Your brain will make it so."

But Imogene seemed like she hadn't even heard Matt. "Almost there, kid. But you gotta hurry."

Now the dam, so to speak, broke. There were too many of them; Matt's wizarding skills—despite the broken wand and his general goofiness—were too strong. They pulled Candelabra apart from Stanbert. They pulled Stanbert apart from Sylvinthia. They overwhelmed even Imogene, who couldn't do enough to stop the onslaught without hurting the kids, which she didn't want to do.

And now Bobert, just as he finished chewing, became as exposed as an actual sloth in the jungle. He only needed the final step of the instructions: to speak out loud to someone else what he wanted most. He just needed to find someone to speak it to, someone not too busy fighting off the horde. Someone to look into his eyes.

Just as the kids descended on him, trying to pin him down, trying to cover his mouth with their hands (they weren't quite clear on the instructions at this point; they just knew they had to stop whatever it was he was doing), Bobert made eye contact with Candelabra. She was being pulled away, almost swallowed up by the crowd. But her face was still out, and she was looking straight at him. And even though he knew he needed to say the words quicker than his current form would allow, he decided to take his time with what he was about to say. He wanted to say it with meaning, not just because he thought it might help the undoing of the spell, but because he thought Candelabra deserved to hear it said truthfully. He deserved to *say* it truthfully, to allow himself to mean it out loud. "I want to be your friend," he said.

At the exact same time, he felt something tug at his fingers, and then Imogene said something he couldn't make out.

AS SOON AS HE FINISHED SAYING THE WORDS, Bobert tried to move his arms to cover his head. It was a purely human instinct (well, maybe it was, like, five percent sloth instinct too), but he was surprised at how quickly he moved to protect himself. He was also surprised by the fact that there weren't any hands on him anymore.

He realized he'd been closing his eyes, and so he opened them again. The first thing he noticed was not that his arms looked like his arms again, but that the sun was about to set. Then he realized how quiet everything was. He sat up, putting on pause his thankfulness to be back in his own body.

Everyone on the parapet looked like they'd just been zapped back into their own bodies. They looked down at their hands, at their feet. Like them, Bobert could feel that something had changed. He felt lighter. Freer.

He also wasn't holding the hair anymore. Not that he ever wanted to hold Matt's hair again. Then he noticed that an

THE BRAVEST WARRIOR IN NEFARIA

adult woman was standing over him, and her fingers on her left hand were pinching something gross and wet. She was big and fairly intimidating, though something about her told him not to be afraid.

As if they realized it at the same moment, all the kids who had been going after him, who had dragged Candelabra and Stanbert off Bobert, let go. They looked around, as if just waking up from a dream.

Everyone was quiet, even Matt.

Bobert looked at the woman again, who offered a smile. She looked around the parapet, and Bobert was wondering if she was someone's mom and had somehow snuck in to rescue her kid. He could remember everything that had happened up until he turned back into himself, so why couldn't he remember who she was?

Then another thought struck him. If he was free, and if the curse had been broken, then there was a chance no one here should know who he was. He looked at Candelabra and Stanbert, who were staring down at themselves, as if they too could feel the new lightness. Then they raised their eyes to meet his and they smiled.

"Are we . . . ?" Stanbert said.

"Who's that?" Candelabra said at the same time.

Bobert's heart sank. It was true. He'd been forgotten. He was going to be cursed forever, forced to follow Matt's every command, and no one he knew would remember he was there.

Then he realized Candelabra was looking past him, at the strange woman. He tried to really look at her and see if any memories came to him, but she was completely unfamiliar to him.

"Do we know you?"

After a silent moment, the woman smiled, then nodded.

"You helped us, didn't you?" Bobert said. "You took the curse." When she didn't say anything, he added on, "Who are you?"

Again the woman didn't answer right away, staring off into the distance as if she needed to gather her thoughts. "I've been called a great warrior," she said. "But I don't know if that was ever true. The greatest warriors aren't just good at fighting battles. They fight for what's right. Me, I was just an instrument." The woman looked directly at Bobert now. "I see that now, thanks to you. You, Bobert, are a greater warrior than I could ever be."

Bobert felt a tear come to his eye, and he reached up to wipe it away. The woman continued, "And if I have to spend my retirement under Matt's control so that you can continue fighting for what's right, so be it."

For some reason, that was the clue the other kids needed to break into action. They let go and started to run away. They ran right past Matt, who also seemed to sense that the spell had dissolved. "Where are you going? No! You are under my control! You do what I say!"

That wasn't very convincing, though, and even Matt knew it. So he did the one thing he knew how to do well (other than complaining and bellowing and exaggerating his own abilities). He reached for his wand.

"Stop him!" Bobert yelled.

But he didn't need to. Even before he'd spoken, the kids near him had knocked the wand out of his hands, and they'd tackled Matt to the ground.

"Take him to the dungeon!" someone shouted. And a loud chorus erupted in agreement.

"What? No!" Matt shouted back, trying to fight them off. But there were too many, and to his misfortune, they had received just enough training to know how to overcome him. Jarrediah had already knocked the wand out of his grip. "There isn't even a dungeon in this castle, probably! Put me down. Put me down and I promise to . . . um . . ."

Within moments he was gone from the parapet, carried off by the army he'd created.

Only Bobert, Stanbert, Candelabra, Sylvinthia, and the mysterious woman remained up there. They looked at one another and started laughing.

"Take care, kids," the woman said. "Nefaria's in good hands with you around." And just like that she headed away, not bothering to explain to them who she was or how she came to be there, just disappearing off somewhere, perhaps never to be seen again.

After that, Bobert found himself wrapped up in a hug. Candelabra had moved in quickly, and the others followed suit. Bobert couldn't imagine a better feeling.

The drawbridge came down. The children who'd been trapped by Matt's gumball machine emerged, free for the first time in years, into a town some of them no longer recognized. The town, however, did not care whether or not they recognized the children.

They greeted them with open arms. They fed them. They offered up their homes, offered up their food, offered up whatever consolation they could provide for the time they'd missed. They rushed into the castle to make sure every kid in Matt's army had a place to sleep, had some measure of comfort that would greet them. Some family members who were still alive found memories coming back to them. And though they could have been overwhelmed by the sudden appearance of these decades-old recollections, though they could have been paralyzed by the tragedy of lost time, they instead went to collect their brothers and sisters and forgotten cousins who'd remained frozen at the age they were when they'd disappeared. They were eager to create new memories with them.

Nefarians managed to get the old king out of his safe room, where they found him weeping over his puzzle. "Sylvinthia," he kept crying. "My daughter. Where is she? Where is she?"

Matt the wizard was left in the dungeon he'd been shoved into to think about what he'd done while he awaited his trial. And though he might have been able to summon Imogene Petunias to break him out, since she was technically under his control, he unfortunately could not remember her.

A few days after the curse ended, Bobert broke away from his friends (*friends!*) to go see Matt in the royal dungeon. He thought again about loneliness, about how it could break the human spirit, and how it hadn't yet broken his. He even said this to Matt, in a not-so-rare-anymore moment of bravery. He said, "I don't think you have to let loneliness break you. You can let it make you better."

Matt the Wizard grumbled for a second, in his way. He patted his robes, reaching for a wand that wasn't there. Bobert wanted to shake his head, or maybe laugh, but he ended up doing neither, just walking back upstairs to go say hi to Sylvinthia.

As it turned out, she had disappeared almost thirty years earlier, when Bobert's parents were kids. Most of the adults recognized her as soon as they saw her, though they were shocked that they hadn't thought of her in so long, shocked that the kingdom had gone on so normally when a princess had gone missing. She was the only gumball kid to stay at the castle, and that first night she helped her dad the king finish a jigsaw puzzle.

Bobert was taking advantage of his newfound visibility. He was still spending a lot of time with his parents, maybe even more than before. But now he had company on his walks to and from school, and his afternoons weren't spent alone. At school he sat with Candelabra, Stanbert, and Jennizabeth at lunch, and all of them begged to trade for his dad's goat stew.

Since he felt more comfortable asking now, Bobert took Stanbert aside and asked him if he remembered the day, months ago, when they'd talked about their favorite sword-swallowers. "Kinda," Stanbert said.

"The next day, you didn't look at me at all," Bobert said, not trying to accuse him. "Do you remember why? It might have just been during my invisible days," he joked.

Stanbert frowned and slurped the rest of his juice box. "The way I remember it, *you* acted like you didn't know *me* at all. So I guess I did the same."

Bobert sat with that for a while, wondering if he had imagined his invisibility the whole time. Had *two* curses been broken that day at the castle? Had the reputation of his bravery earned him friends? Or was he simply braver now, more willing to let himself be seen?

The Council of Elders, who were the first to admit that their protocols left a lot to be desired, all resigned. They were not doing enough to protect Nefaria from evil schemes, they said, and obviously they had not reacted in time to the evil scheme that had unfolded. Nefaria would choose new Elders, or they would come up with a new system entirely.

But that would come later. First, the town and the king-dom breathed easy. They allowed themselves the joy of an evil scheme foiled. They knew it would not be the last. They knew they would have to stay vigilant. They would have to fight back again, sometime in the future. But for now there was time for relaxation and celebration.

Two weeks after Matt's brief rule ended, everyone gathered in the town square. There was food and dancing and music. They didn't just celebrate the children's freedom. They cele-brated the fact that it was the children who had freed them-selves, the children who had squashed the evil scheme before the adults even knew what to do about it. Maybe the solution to evil schemes was to not leave the grown-ups in charge all the time.

Maybe that could have helped Candelabra's sister not get stuck in the painting. Maybe it would help Candelabra moving forward to take matters into her own hands, and not wait for adults to act.

For now, though, she celebrated.

A lot of the gumball children threw themselves into celebration. They feasted on food. Food they hadn't tasted in so long. They drank as much carbonated sugar water as they pleased, ate candy by the fistful until they were sick. But it was a good kind of feeling sick, holding their stomachs, moaning about a pain and a discomfort that was so temporary that it felt almost silly, especially because they were living through it with others.

Other children wanted only to sleep. When their ordeal had ended, they had asked for the nearest bed, and they'd buried themselves beneath the sheets, happy knowing no one was going to wake them up in the morning by banging on a pan. They were happy knowing that they would get to choose when to wake up, and what to do with themselves once that had happened. Some were still sleeping the day of the feast.

Bobert, Candelabra, Jennizabeth, and Stanbert went to the bench where they'd gathered that fateful afternoon, across from where the gumball machine used to be. For a long time they just sat. Jarrediah came to join them, for a little while, before he was tempted back by his sisters (older now, but still annoying) to the food stands that had popped up all over the square.

They watched the town throw its joy around, joy they had given it. Joy that was deep within them, too, even if right now it looked a little different.

Bobert was the first to speak. "Hey, do you guys believe in

that curse about the pinball machine in the play hall?"

Candelabra smacked his arm with the back of her hand, and Stanbert shouted for him to shut up. Bobert laughed. "Kidding, kidding."

"Didn't know you were so funny," Jennizabeth said.

"We didn't know much about you in general," Candelabra said.

Some fireworks shot out from nearby, whooshing in that satisfying whistling way they had, then popping overhead with bursts of red and green and white. In between the explosions, music from the stage carried over, and the roar of Nefaria celebrating.

"We should change that, though," Candelabra said.

"Change what?" Bobert asked. He'd forgotten what they'd been talking about.

"How much we know about each other. We're friends, after all."

Bobert turned to look at Candelabra, almost wishing he were a sloth again, just so his smile would feel like the natural state of his face. Then he realized it didn't matter if Candelabra knew he was smiling. Actually, he was glad she would know that what she said made him happy.

"I know," he said.

Another burst of fireworks, and all of Nefaria seemed to be alight with joy, and celebration, and happiness. The crowd at the square let out whoops and laughs.

The group of friends fell quiet again, not feeling the need to say anything else.

And so it was. The kingdom prone to both evil and beauty survived one and embraced the other.

ACKNOWLEDGMENTS

FIRST OF ALL, thanks to Laura Fairbank for demanding a bedtime story, then providing a prompt when I rudely refused. It helped you sleep, and everything else is icing on the cake.

People who helped make it a cake, though:

Pete Knapp, as always, along with Stuti Telidevara. Jessi Smith for helping weave together my fevered bedtime ramblings/jokes/Nanowrimo project into a cohesive story in a more cohesive world. Thanks to the entire Aladdin team for obliging me in my silliness and putting this book out into the world.

Thanks to Jeff Miller for being an early reader and meeting up for writing sessions and pandemic walks.

Thanks to Remy, who's the best inspiration/distraction for many bedtime stories to come.

Thanks to my family, for everything.

ABOUT THE AUTHOR

Born and raised in Mexico City, **ADI ALSAID** is the author of several young adult novels including *Let's Get Lost*, *We Didn't Ask For This*, and *North of Happy*, a Kirkus Best Book nominee. He currently lives in Chicago with his wife, son, and two cats, where he occasionally spills hot sauce on things and cats (but at the time of this writing, not yet on his son). This is his first middle grade novel.